Praise for Geoff Nicholson and *Female Ruins*

'Geoff Nicholson knows his architecture . . . His knowledge of the subject is sure, his understanding of the design and theories of the past thirty years assured and enjoyably related. None of this, however, should or does get in the way of his very human storytelling: it is there as point and counterpoint to the underlying thrust of *Female Ruins*' *Guardian*

'A clever post-modern story, well told'
Times Literary Supplement

'*Female Ruins* is a treat, both for its writing and its heroine' *Marie Claire*

'Nicholson's writing is rife with deadpan wit, a style that brings both warmth to his characters and a chill to their obsessions' *Arena*

'Highly original' *Time Out*

'Nicholson doesn't just give you what you want, he gives you what you never even knew existed'
Independent on Sunday

Geoff Nicholson was born in Sheffield. His novels include *Hunters and Gatherers, Everything and More, Footsucker, Bleeding London*, which was shortlisted for the Whitbread Award, and *Flesh Guitar*. His works have been translated into French, German, Japanese, Italian and Spanish. He lives in London and New York.

BY THE SAME AUTHOR

FICTION

Street Sleeper
Still Life with Volkswagens
The Knot Garden
What We Did on our Holidays
Hunters and Gatherers
The Food Chain
The Errol Flynn Novel
Everything and More
Footsucker
Bleeding London
Flesh Guitar

NON-FICTION

Big Noises
Day Trips to the Desert

Female Ruins

GEOFF NICHOLSON

PHŒNIX

A PHOENIX PAPERBACK

First published in Great Britain by Victor Gollancz in 1999
This paperback edition published in 2000 by Phoenix,
an imprint of Orion Books Ltd,
Orion House, 5 Upper St Martin's Lane,
London WC2H 9EA

A CIP catalogue record for this book
is available from the British Library.

ISBN: 0 75380 916 8

Printed and bound in Great Britain by
The Guernsey Press Co. Ltd, Guernsey, C.I.

I

THE OLD WORLD

'More simply, ruin is part of the general *Weltschmertz, Sehnsucht*, malaise, nostalgia, angst, frustration, sickness, passion of the human soul; it is the eternal symbol. Literature and art have always carried it; it has had as a fashion its ups and downs, but the constant mood and appetite is there.'

Rose Macaulay, *Pleasures of Ruin*

'Am I wrong, or are fewer and fewer people using the word *Weltschmerz* these days?'

Christopher Howell, *The Ruins of Pleasure*

1

Some nights she wouldn't even have bothered to pick up the phone. The last train up from London got into Carsham station at ten-thirty and most of the time nobody got off at all, and even when somebody did get off, the chances were they wouldn't be needing a taxi. But just in case they did, Kelly's card was displayed in the window of the closed and deserted station office. And if the phone rang, and if she wasn't too tired or apathetic or pissed or stoned, then she would answer it, say, 'Kelly's Cabs' (even though there was only one), and get in her car and go pick up a fare and drive them home through the dark, empty Suffolk roads. But this time the call came at half-past eleven, which she considered way too late, and at first she wasn't going to answer it at all, but the phone kept ringing, wouldn't go away, and she eventually made herself grab the receiver.

She didn't say her name at first. She knew it could all too easily be some drunk on the other end of the line, and she wanted them to speak so she could judge whether they sounded like trouble. But a sober, polite, somewhat hesitant male voice with a soft American accent asked if she was the 'car service' and she said she wasn't quite sure what that meant, but yes, she drove a taxi, if that's what he was looking for.

The man on the phone said the train had arrived late and he was stranded at Carsham station, and was there any way she could come and pick him up? He asked very nicely indeed and said that he would understand perfectly if she didn't want to turn out at that time of night, but he said it in a way that made it impossible for her to refuse. She said OK.

She put on her leopardskin jacket, got in her car, drove the three miles from her home to the station, and there in the car park she saw a tall, lost-looking American. She wasn't sure how, but you could tell his nationality just from his appearance. He was wearing chinos and a button-down Oxford shirt and an expensive, creased linen jacket. They were all clothes that an Englishman could have worn, but this man wore them differently, in a way that advertised his foreignness.

He looked boyish, but he was the kind of man who, she suspected, would still look boyish when he was sixty. She guessed he was a little older than her, a whisker over thirty, whereas she was a significant whisker under. It was his lean-ness, his gangliness that made him appear young. He looked as though he lived unhappily in his own body. There was something staid about him, something strained, that she found unattractive, but she immediately forced herself to stop thinking in those terms. Times were bad indeed when she had to think about her passengers in terms of their sexual desirability, but she knew this already. It had been a bad year, a bad few years.

She pulled up next to him, observed that his luggage was fancy and expensive, wound down her window and asked him where he wanted to be taken; he said the Phoenix Inn. She laughed. He looked confused and explained it was a local pub where he had a room reserved. Did she know where it was? Indeed she did. It was situated all of a hundred and fifty yards away from the station. She pointed in its direction. You could almost see it from where they were. She was annoyed at the waste of time for so little potential reward, and didn't feel inclined to pretend otherwise. The man looked crestfallen, and then like a child with an embarrassing confession he pointed down at his right leg, which she could now see was bent at a peculiar angle, and she saw too that there was a walking stick leaning against one of the cases. It was an elaborate thing, lacquered glossy black, its head carved into the shape of a crocodile, its jaws wide open in the act of swallowing a naked woman, whose head, shoulders and breasts were still visible. Kelly wondered what the hell that was supposed to mean.

'OK, no problem,' she said. It wasn't quite an apology, just an acceptance that, yes, he did need a taxi after all.

She put his bags in the back of the car and offered to help him into his seat, but he said he could take care of himself. He insisted on sitting up front beside her, partly as a gesture of egalitarianism, but there was more leg room there anyway. She waited until he was settled and then drove him slowly and majestically the laughably short distance to the pub. There was hardly time for conversation but she was aware of him looking around the inside of the car, inspecting it, and there was just time for him to remark that she was young and female and to ask whether it wasn't dangerous for her to be driving a taxi at this time of night.

'This is rural Suffolk,' she said. 'Not New York.'

By then they'd got to the pub and pulled into the gravel driveway. 'Nice looking place,' he said. It was an old, wood-framed Tudor coaching inn. Parts of it were authentically old but it had been tarted up and painted in stark black and

11

white that had the effect of making it look authentically ersatz.

'You'll see better,' Kelly said.

She unloaded the bags and carried them to the front door of the pub for him. The place was locked but there were lights on inside and she rang the bell and waited for someone to open up. Her passenger said he was really sorry to have dragged her out for such a ridiculously short trip, and she appreciated that at least he recognized the absurdity of the situation. On the other hand, she supposed there was no way he'd have got to the Phoenix Inn without her. He asked for her business card, which she handed over, and he paid his fare and said keep the change. She could hear the landlord arriving to unlock the door of the pub, and she returned to her car. She checked the money she'd been given and saw that the tip was only just on the right side of generous.

Next morning, before nine, Kelly's phone rang again. This time she answered at once, thinking she was back to her old working routine, but she heard the same American voice she'd heard late last night.

'Hi, this is Dexter,' he said, 'Jack Dexter, the limping American.' He paused, as if waiting for her to be amused by this bit of self-deprecation. When it didn't come he continued, 'Although, for some reason, everybody just calls me Dexter. I'm still sorry about dragging you out last night.'

'It's all right,' she said. 'I'm a taxi driver, that's how I make my living. Although I wouldn't make much of one if all my trips were like last night's. What can I do for you?'

He said he needed her services again, and he launched into what seemed to her an unnecessary bout of autobiography, but perhaps, she thought, that was the American way.

He explained that he was in England on a two-week vacation. He was recently divorced from his wife and needed some time away. His plan had been to hire a car and tour the area, but a few days before leaving home he'd had this terrible problem with his leg, the flaring up of an old knee injury. It was too painful to allow him to drive. Cancelling the holiday would have been admitting defeat, so he'd made up his mind to come anyway, but now he was stuck in the Phoenix Inn in Carsham without any transport. He said he wanted her and her car to be at his disposal for the next seven days. What was her going rate?

'Hold on,' said Kelly. 'What are we talking about here? What exactly does "at your disposal" mean? How many hours of the day or night? What sort of distances?'

'Oh well,' he muttered. He sounded flustered, surprised, as though he was unaccustomed to having people ask him to explain himself. Then, rapidly, he said, 'I guess I was thinking of a series of day trips. You know, some of them just there and back, some maybe circular journeys, some triangular maybe.'

'Where to?' she asked.

'Just the immediate area,' he said. 'Just sightseeing, tourist stuff, nothing too difficult. There wouldn't be any really long drives. I just want to get to see the area. It might be a bit boring for you. And I guess I might need a little help getting up and down flights of stairs, but I'm not an invalid, I'm not asking you to be my nurse or anything like that.'

'That's just as well,' said Kelly.

She did some swift, only partially competent, mental arithmetic, tried to form an equation that combined an hourly rate with a price per mile and came up with a figure. If he'd accepted it immediately she'd have thought he was an idiot,

13

just a stupid American tourist with too much money, but he haggled with her, brought the price down a bit, and she rather respected him for that.

Even so, she was sure that on other occasions she'd have flatly said she wasn't interested in the job. For one thing, if he was going to employ her for the whole week then there were a couple of regular fares she'd need to cancel or work round, and that was going to be a hassle. Furthermore, spending a whole week with somebody she didn't know could be asking for trouble. Dexter seemed unobjectionable, but her acquaintance with him ran to about four minutes, and she knew she wasn't the most tolerant or easy-going person. So there were good reasons for turning down the job, but in the event she accepted it, and before too long she thought she'd worked out her real motivation. As she was making arrangements for when she would pick him up at the Phoenix Inn later that morning and where she would drive him, she realized she was taking this job because in some peculiar way Dexter reminded her of her late father.

For a long time Kelly had been very polite to people who came asking questions about her father. She had wanted to be helpful. She told them what she knew, but it was never enough for them. They wanted answers and information that she didn't have. They wanted her to tell them things she couldn't possibly know. They made her feel inadequate and ashamed; not exactly new feelings for her. She felt that a good daughter should have known more, should have had more insight. But what was she to do? She was only thirteen when her father died and, although she'd spent a lot of time thinking about him and wondering how things might have been if he'd lived, by and large she'd resisted the temptation to turn herself into a scholar of her father's life and times.

She'd left that to the others, to the ones who came asking questions.

Her father's name was Christopher Howell, a name that meant next to nothing in the world at large, but which rang a loud, occasionally alarming bell in certain small, tight architectural circles. In these places people could get oddly excited at the mention of his name. He was someone people didn't feel neutral about. He was a cult figure of sorts. And, if you believed a monograph written in the late eighties, he was 'the greatest modern English architect never to have built a building'. Others said he was just a trifler, a poseur and a fraud.

At the heart of her father's reputation were three quirky books about architecture. They consisted of strange, short, sometimes witty, sometimes gnomic, often semi-autobiographical essays about architecture. The first was called *Watch it Come Up*, the second was *Buckminster Fuller's Bedspread* and the third *The Ruins of Pleasure*. They had been published in the middle and late seventies, and all were still intermittently in print, and still read by the cooler sort of architectural students. He wrote about quirky things: ice houses, domestic garages, metal buildings, the design of crazy golf courses; writing seriously about unserious architecture

There was also a collection of drawings, consisting of plans and artist's impressions of projects that her father had dreamed up. A few of them were fully realized drawings, but most were little more than doodles. Her father hadn't been much of a draughtsman, even less of an artist and the drawings were scrappy, hairy things, but they had a crude, spirited charm about them.

Some of the schemes invented or depicted in his work might just conceivably have been built, given a massively wealthy and massively indulgent patron. Others were pure fantasy: vast buildings constructed on tiny stilts, suburbs laid out according to arcane and ironic principles, cities of the future waiting for a technology that would make them possible.

The story was that her father never found a patron, indulgent or otherwise, and since he couldn't make his ideas concrete, he'd decided to make them as abstract as possible. He became a sort of architectural philosopher, a propagator of 'speculative architecture', a genius figure to some, almost a guru to one or two.

Some of the people who appreciated her father's work said that the impracticality of his ideas, the essential unbuildableness of his buildings, was the whole point. Their beauty, they said, lay in their impracticality, their lavishness, their irony. Some just said they were works of art, poetic inventions. Kelly was very happy with this view.

Other critics said that, even though he'd done his training at the Architectural Association, her father had never really intended or wanted to be an architect. They said his self-assigned role was to act as a sort of philosophical whetstone, someone against whom students and scholars, and even architects, could hone themselves and their ideas, thereby becoming sharper and more cutting edge.

Kelly would have found this last proposition utterly depressing if she'd thought it was true, but she didn't think it was. From what she could remember of her father, and from reading his books, he had seemed desperate to create buildings, real buildings, not just flights of fancy, not just works on paper. Even as a child she had recognized that in him, and her mother, on the rare occasions when she could be induced to talk about him, remembered his frustrated ambition far more than she remembered his genius.

Kelly's mother stopped giving interviews long before Kelly

did. She had no desire to become the caring, protective widow. It would have been quite possible for her to style herself as the guardian of her late husband's reputation and legacy. But she had quickly decided that was a mug's game.

It took Kelly much longer. She kept giving time to earnest young scholars. They came from all over the world and many of them seemed nice and conscientious enough, and she tried to please them. She tried to come up with something they could use, some extra memory, some undiscovered letter or drawing. But before long everything she was prepared to give had become extant, had entered the public domain. The ones who came next quickly realized that. They found her useless, of no interest, an empty vessel, and that depressed her. At first she wasn't sure why. After all, these people were strangers, they meant nothing to her. But then she knew there had been many times when her father had also found her useless and of no interest. By being of interest to scholars, and in talking about her father, she had doubly tried to redeem herself.

The bare bones of her relationship with her father were easily summed up. Even though her parents were conventional enough to be married, they both liked to think of themselves as free spirits. They may have had a piece of paper from the City Hall, actually the Chelsea Town Hall, but they didn't feel tied. In fact, so untrammelled did her father feel that the moment Kelly was conceived he was up and gone. Her mother took it pretty well. She didn't want to restrict his genius, she said, and anyway what was the point of trying to keep someone who didn't want to be kept? They eventually got divorced but the break was not absolute. Throughout the early years of Kelly's life, out of guilt as much as out of affection, she suspected, her father would make sporadic reappearances, make ever more incompetent

17

attempts to be a good father to her and a good partner to her mother, before leaving again. Kelly couldn't claim that she ever felt unloved exactly and it was easy to imagine infinitely worse, infinitely less efficient fathers, but she could never escape the pain and puzzlement, the feeling of impending abandonment. She always knew that he had other, grander, more important things on his mind than his daughter; and that hurt.

Her mother showed Kelly her father's articles when they appeared in magazines or newspapers. She remembered watching him in a debate on television about the future of cities. And then she remembered the obituaries. Some of them were warm, some of them were sneering; but either way they suggested that her father was someone who had to be dealt with. She noticed how much they got wrong. One obituary said he was happily married with one son, another said he'd never married at all. She supposed that was all part of the myth; contradictory data that some swot would think was worth delving into. She remembered being surprisingly, incomprehensibly unmoved by the immediate fact of his death. Only years later did it get to her.

In his occasional autobiographical writings her father sometimes described himself as a drop out, as an ageing hippie, as a bum; but she knew he was only playing with the words. He meant that he'd never had a 'proper job', that money wasn't exactly plentiful, that he didn't lead a conventional middle-class life. It was true in a way, but there was a lot wrong with that picture. For one thing he worked hard, far too hard ever to be considered a drop out. And yes, money was a struggle, but there were always bursaries and grants and lecture trips abroad, and when he came to see Kelly and her mother there were usually expensive presents. And while he didn't have a mortgage or his own house,

18

he was very good at finding rich people who would invite him to house-sit for them, who were happy to have him stay in their guest house, their holiday cottage, their Georgian gate lodge.

It was left to Kelly to be the true failure of the family. She sometimes felt she lived her life by negatives. As she got older it seemed to her that her father had been both blessed and cursed by his calling: blessed in that he knew with great precision what he wanted to do with his life; cursed in that he was never able to do it. Her own problem, it seemed to her, was that she had never discovered what it was she wanted to do. She occasionally thought she ought to try to live up to her father's reputation and (disputed) genius. She wouldn't have objected to following in his footsteps, trying to succeed in the areas in which he'd failed, making his ambitions hers, but she knew that wasn't on. She knew she hadn't inherited any of her father's gifts – for inventing, for writing, for thinking. She never wanted to be an architect but she also knew she'd never have had the opportunity. She was sure she didn't want to go to university, sure she didn't want to be in the public eye, didn't want to make masses of money; but again it would have been all the same if she *had* wanted to. She had no talent in those directions. Sometimes she felt as though she had no talent at all.

Early on she'd decided that she wanted to be good with her hands, but she hadn't wanted to do anything girlie, hadn't wanted to throw pots or screw around with batik. She studied woodwork, thought she might become a crafts-woman, a cabinet-maker, be good at marquetry or hand-carving or something, but she was never better than average. Then for a while she was an average painter and decorator, the real thing with emulsion and wallpaper, not some sort of tricksy interior designer. She even tried her hand at laying floors and tiling bathrooms, but she found she was average at that too.

She supposed that if you had to psychoanalyse this stuff you'd have said that whereas her father's work had been nebulous and theoretical, she deliberately chose work that was solid and substantial; but it hadn't seemed that way at the time. Mostly she was just trying to make a living as best she could. 'But if you think that makes me sound like an underachiever,' she'd say, 'you should have seen me when I was fifteen.'

She'd had a few bad years after her father died, nothing truly spectacular, just the usual mild transgressions that teenage girls are capable of: shoplifting, sex with older boys, Class B drugs. Her mother was helpless, her school was pathetic. There were counsellors and briefly a therapist, and she had a lot of fun pissing them off, sitting in stony silence for a whole hour-long session being one of her favourite techniques. She guessed they saw she was a well brought up girl at heart and that she'd eventually sort herself out. And she had. She got caught in a stolen car with a bunch of extremely dodgy 25-year-olds, got threatened with every imaginable legal and social indignity (and her imagination was pretty good in those days), and without a great deal of fuss she'd cleaned up her act, not completely, she hadn't become a born-again virgin, but had cleaned it up enough to stay out of court. It had not really been any big deal, she said now. But if you'd seen her aged fifteen, a joint in one hand, a bottle of vodka in the other, some yob's hand up her shirt, you'd have thought that ending up as a jobbing carpenter or painter and decorator was more than she had any right to expect.

Then she gave that up too. Working with her hands was not the joy she had hoped it would be. She saw that solidity

20

was not necessarily to be found in building materials. So she became a taxi driver. She liked it. It suited her. It wasn't practical, it wasn't creative, but that was all right because it wasn't meant to be.

She had always liked driving. It made her feel independent, not free exactly, but certainly released. It was mood changing, consciousness altering. Driving fast was undoubtedly a thrill, but in her bit of Suffolk that wasn't always possible. The roads were full of fearful old ladies and gents who felt that driving at thirty miles an hour on straight, open roads somehow kept them safe and gave them longer lives.

She liked driving fast at night through the tight curves of deserted country lanes; the hedges rising beside her, the narrow tunnel of landscape being revealed, being called into existence by the high beam of her headlights. She liked being in control and yet on automatic pilot. She loved the way driving relied on instinct as much as conscious skill, and it always pleased her to arrive somewhere in her car and have only the vaguest memories of the drive there.

In her time she'd owned sporty little convertibles and funky old classics, but she'd also owned vans and a Ford Transit, and driving them was good too. But when she decided to become a taxi driver she bought an oldish, high-spec Volvo estate car. It was so respectable, so middle-aged, so unlike herself, and perhaps that was why she liked to wear the leopardskin jacket; it fulfilled a need to subvert the expectations of what Volvo drivers, let alone taxi drivers, should be like. And she liked to have music blasting out of the stereo; loud passionate music by loud passionate women, Bessie Smith and Patti Smith, Babes in Toyland and Hole – all Americans she realized.

She never pretended that driving a taxi was interesting or fulfilling, but it was honest and regular. She took people to

21

and from the station, she took old ladies on shopping trips; later she might take them to the hospital. She sometimes took drunks home after the pubs were shut, but she tried to avoid that. She could deal with drunks all right, but she didn't want to have to clean up their vomit. It wasn't exactly Travis Bickle stuff, though of course you got fares who had sex on their way home, sluts who let themselves be groped and fucked on the back seat of the car. That was usually all right by her. The seat covers were stain resistant. She just kept driving and kept her eye on things in the rearview mirror. There were days when it was titillating, when it seemed like the best part of the job, when it seemed that just by driving her car she was part of some shared universal erotic impulse. But there were other days when it made her feel so depressed, so lonely, days when she wished she could be the slut on the back seat.

2

Kelly drove to the Phoenix Inn and collected Dexter. The itinerary he'd worked out for that first day was undemanding to the point of stupor. Kelly was to drive him to Southwold, then to Aldeburgh, a simple round trip up and down the coast, not more than forty miles all told. She was aware that lots of people thought these places were fascinating little towns, wonderful holiday spots. They said how clean and neat and well-ordered and English they were. She wouldn't have argued with that, but she'd known them, hung around in them, been bored in them, for most of her life, and the magic had long since worn off.

Still, a job was a job. In Southwold she could show Dexter the lighthouse, the cannons that pointed out to sea ready to repel Dutch invaders, the open greens created by historic fires in the town, the sailors' reading room. In Aldeburgh she could show him the harbour, the new lifeboat station, the Martello Tower. She knew these were acceptable as 'sights' but they didn't exactly excite her, and unless Dexter was a very cold fish indeed she couldn't see that they were likely to excite him either.

He was waiting for her in the car park. He was overdressed, as though he was setting off on a major expedition. He wore a down-filled jacket, carried a rucksack, had state-of-the-art walking boots. Someone must have told him how bad the English weather was. In fact, the day was mild and bright, a good October day.

He arranged himself, his bad leg and his walking stick in the car and looked around it as though still inspecting for faults. Kelly always kept the car neat and clean, so she hadn't had to make any special effort in Dexter's honour, but his perusal was so fussy, so imperious, she rather wished she'd arranged some mess or litter especially to irritate him.

When he'd completed the visual inspection, he said approvingly, 'It's a nice clean cab. I could tell right away you weren't a smoker, and I'm really pleased you don't use any of those synthetic air fresheners.'

'Good morning,' Kelly said. 'Nice day, isn't it?'

Then Dexter seemed to remember that people didn't always begin their conversations with remarks about the neatness of cars.

'Oh, OK,' he said. 'I was forgetting I'm in England. We have to discuss the weather, right?'

Kelly was about to say that they didn't have to talk about anything at all as far as she was concerned, but before she could speak, his eyes fell on the stack of cassettes she kept in the car. They too were neat and clean and kept in a snug little rack between the gear lever and the hand brake. Dexter looked at them dubiously, read the titles and grimaced. Kelly couldn't see what he was looking offended about. She never forced her musical preferences on her passengers. She knew that Lydia Lunch was an acquired taste, that Seven Year Bitch weren't for everyone. She only ever played them when she was alone in the cab before or after she'd had a fare. But just the appearance, the mere existence of her tape collection seemed to disturb Dexter.

'Don't you like classical music?' he asked.

'I don't know much about it.'

'Me neither,' he admitted, 'but I'm trying to learn.'

He reached in through the layers that encased his body and pulled out a cassette. She could read the name Bach on the box.

'Perhaps this week could be an education for both of us,' he said. 'Johann Sebastian Bach, born Eisenach, Germany, sixteen eighty-five.'

He proceeded to give her a brief rundown on the life and times of J. S. Bach, and although she wasn't really listening she caught something about 'polyphonic baroque'. It sounded as though he was quoting liner notes. Then, without asking, he put his tape into the car's cassette player. Kelly was annoyed, but the music that came out was inoffensive enough.

'Is this your first time in England?' she asked.

'No, my fifth.'

'You must like it.'

'Yes, I suppose I must.'

'Where in America do you come from?'

'California. Los Angeles.'

'Really? You're not my idea of a Californian.'

'You think I should be riding a skateboard?'

'I suppose I thought you'd be more laidback.'

'I work very hard not to be laidback. I work pretty hard at trying not to appear Californian.'

'I think Suffolk might seem a little bit tame after Los Angeles.'

'I can see why you might think that,' Dexter agreed. 'But frankly, any damn fool can be impressed by Los Angeles. Just like anyone can be impressed by New York or Chicago or Niagara Falls. To appreciate the pleasures of England takes more subtlety. I'm quite into subtlety.'

Yes, I bet you are, Kelly thought.

He wound down the window as they drove, and he pressed his face into the wind like a dog. He seemed quite happy for a moment. They got to Southwold, the sort of place any sightseer would need to view on foot, but Dexter was obviously in no condition to tramp the streets. Kelly did her best to show him the town by car but it was a partial and unsatisfactory tour. This was not a town laid out for cruising. After she'd done her best she drove to the seafront, parked, got Dexter out of the car and escorted him to a bench where he could sit and gaze down at the sea and the beach huts some way below. Wild times, indeed.

It was then that Kelly realized she was treating him like an old, infirm relative, one possibly not long for this world, and she saw how absurd this was. Dexter was a strong, healthy-looking man, not much older than she, who happened to have a bad leg. His infirmity was both localized and temporary.

'How's your leg?' she asked.

'Kind of irritating,' he replied, as he settled himself sideways into the corner of the bench and extended his leg out in front of him.

'Is it very painful?'

'Yes, sometimes it is. Which is in itself irritating.'

She sat at the other end of the bench and looked out over the water. The sea and sky were unseasonably blue. An oil tanker moved ponderously across the horizon and in the sea, much nearer, someone in an inflatable dinghy with an outboard motor was turning figures of eight. A tawny cat was climbing painstakingly over the roofs of the beach huts.

'What are those things?'

'Beach huts,' said Kelly. 'They're little places where you change in and out of your swimming costume, where you make cups of tea, where you sit and eat cucumber sandwiches and read Agatha Christie novels.'

'Simple English pleasures,' said Dexter.

'Yes,' Kelly said, feeling some need to defend them. 'I like their simplicity, their colours, their names.'

'They have names?'

'Yes. People call them things like "Avocets" or "Klondike" or "Sleepy Hollow".'

'You can sleep in them?'

'Only in the day time. Not at night. You're not allowed to spend the night there. I think they're afraid hippies might move in and set up some sort of immoral commune. This way you can be immoral but only when it's light outside.'

Dexter gave her a look that she couldn't read. She wondered if he was offended by her casual talk of immorality. It didn't seem very likely, but either way she didn't feel repentant. If he was offended that easily the world must be a very hurtful place indeed. She talked a little more about beach huts, how expensive they were to buy, how they couldn't be used for one month of each year because of some legal requirement, and how, even in a place as civilized and well-ordered as Southwold, a few bad youths would occasionally go crazy and burn one of them down.

Dexter showed polite interest but it seemed to her he was faking. The conversation petered out and they sat in silence. It was the sort of mild, comfortable day when two people might well sit on a bench in silence and be quite content, but that wasn't how it felt to Kelly, and apparently it didn't feel that way to Dexter either, since he said suddenly, 'You could leave me alone here for a while. I have a book with me, *Don Quixote*, as a matter of fact. You don't have to be my constant companion, you know."

It could have been said generously and considerately but

in fact it sounded like an insult, a complaint. Kelly was happy to go. She went down to the seafront and walked past the huts, but as she wandered along, an unfamiliar guilt came over her. She knew that feeling sorry for someone wasn't the most noble of emotions but she tried to put herself in Dexter's place; in a strange country, broken up from his wife, injured, immobile, with nobody except a taxi driver to talk to, and she thought he had every reason to be thoroughly, hopelessly miserable. She in turn decided to be charitable and make that an excusable cause of his tetchy, awkward behaviour, and she resolved to try harder. She didn't stay away for very long, and when she got back to the bench she attempted to make conversation.

'Is Bach your favourite composer?' she asked.

He shrugged. 'He was my wife's favourite. Well, I suppose he still is.'

Kelly tried to imagine what his wife might be like, and could only come up with a mental picture of some sort of standard-issue, blonde California beach babe.

'No girlfriend?' she asked.

She didn't think it was too personal a question, given how free Dexter had been with information, but he reacted as though she had demanded to know something indecently intimate.

'I don't have anyone who was prepared to come on vacation with me to England if that's what you're asking,' he said.

She hadn't been aware she was asking that at all, but now it did seem to be a significant piece of information, the more so since Dexter said it as though it were a terrible admission of failure and inadequacy.

'Besides,' he said, now attempting to smooth over this little ripple of self-revelation, 'travelling's more interesting alone. You see things differently. You put yourself at risk. Things happen to you that wouldn't happen if you were with somebody else.'

Kelly nodded. She took the point, though she didn't see what kind of adventure was likely to happen to a person sitting on a bench in Southwold reading *Don Quixote*. Dexter looked around him at the perfectly calm, uneventful English seascape, at the old people walking by, at the café offering 'beach trays' and he said with finality, 'This place isn't so bad.'

'It's fine,' Kelly agreed.

'But I think I'm ready to move on.'

So they drove to Aldeburgh, some fifteen miles down the coast, where it was more of the same. Kelly drove through the town, pointing out the landmarks such as they were, and when that was accomplished she drove to a spot where Dexter could sit on the sea wall and stay out of harm's way. She did her best to be chatty without being intrusive, but it was hard work and she felt she was the one making most of the effort. Then Dexter decided he was hungry.

'I like to have fish and chips at least once while I'm in England,' he said.

Feeling only somewhat like a drudge, Kelly went and queued up for fish and chips and brought them back. Dexter said they were fine but he behaved as though he were eating some dangerous and exotic delicacy dredged up from the darkest corner of the known world. Time was passing. The day was gradually being worn away, but for Kelly the slowness of the process was an ordeal. She felt she was really earning her money.

'You English,' said Dexter, 'with your batter and your chips and your malt vinegar; very, very inscrutable.'

Kelly didn't react to that one. When they'd finished eating

29

she was commanded to leave him again, and as she walked away Dexter said, 'Perhaps while you're gone you might buy something for me?'

'All right.'

'A souvenir.'

'What kind of souvenir?'

'Anything you like. Just a little something that will remind me of this day.'

Kelly frowned. Who would want reminding? Besides, she suspected he would dislike anything she chose. With that in mind, and with no emotional investment in the purchase, she went to a craftshop in the high street and bought him a little model of a beach hut. It was wooden, painted in bright colours, big enough to sit in the palm of the hand.

She took her time returning. She could see Dexter from a long way off. He'd stopped reading his book and was sitting dejectedly, head down, arms folded. And as she watched, he took a silver hip flask out of his pocket and took a long, eager swig from it. She found that touchingly human. She made sure he had time to put the flask away before she got close, and when he saw her he smiled with an unexpectedly open and boyish expression and she found it quite beguiling. She handed him the paper bag containing the model beach hut. He opened the bag, looked inside, and his smile was gone. His face showed nothing she could understand, not amusement, not surprise, certainly not appreciation.

'How much did it cost?' he asked.

'Don't worry,' Kelly said. 'It's on the house.'

'Really, I have to pay you.'

'You really don't.'

'No, I couldn't take a gift from you.'

'Keep it, for God's sake,' Kelly said.

This was a brand-new form of irritation. His capacity for gracelessness knew no bounds. He could turn a simple, friendly gesture into a source of conflict.

'Forget it,' Kelly said. 'Just forget it. In fact why don't we both forget the whole thing. This has been a bad day for both of us. We don't need this. You could find yourself a much more sympathetic tour guide than me, I'm sure.'

Dexter was silent and he looked at her with big, vacant, wounded eyes.

'This hasn't been a bad day for me,' he said. 'I've enjoyed it a lot. I've really enjoyed your company.'

That made her feel even worse, though she suspected he wanted her to feel that way.

'I'm sorry,' Kelly said.

'And I'm sorry too, sorry if I've bored you,' he said. 'Perhaps you should have taken me somewhere *you* wanted to go.'

Kelly tried to apologize again.

'No really,' said Dexter, 'I mean it. How about this for a deal? Before the day ends, take me somewhere that isn't in the guide books.'

'I don't know you,' Kelly said. 'I don't know what sort of thing you like.'

'It doesn't matter what I like. Take me somewhere *you* like.'

Kelly considered this for a moment and then said OK. She thought she had nothing to lose. She loaded Dexter back into the car and began to drive.

Most people were surprised when Kelly said she loved visiting parish churches. They had to be small, human in scale, perhaps a bit eccentric. At their best they stirred something profound in her; not a belief in God, but a belief in humanity. The knowledge that she was standing in a spot where people had congregated for centuries, surrounded by stonework that still bore the marks of medieval craftsmen was somehow very moving. There was a sense of continuity, connectedness, the living with the dead. She knew it was out of character. She knew that a taxi driver who liked ear-bleed music wasn't expected to have these feelings, but she did, and they wouldn't go away.

She knew it had a lot to do with her father. His idea of a good day out was getting into the car, handing her a volume of Pevsner and having her read out architectural descriptions until they came to some particularly choice round-towered church or leper chapel. From the earliest age she remembered him teaching her the names of architectural features. Perhaps she wasn't the only ten-year-old whose vocabulary included words like corbel, piscina, misericord, flushwork, clerestory, but she had never met another.

She took Dexter to the church of St Margaret at Dunstan. She'd taken a lot of people there and, no doubt unjustly, she tended to judge them by their reaction to the place. The church was small, and the outside a bit of a mess; a patchwork of replastering and rendering in all sorts of unmatching colours, blistering greys and curdled oranges. It had thick buttresses, big, crude functional triangles of stone that kept the walls up. The church was simple inside, a nave and one aisle and that was pretty much it. It was cool, had a high wooden ceiling, plain pews, a square stone font. But her reason for taking people there was not so much the architecture as the decoration.

Kelly and Dexter walked down the nave, between the rows of pews with their home-crocheted kneelers, until they came to the rood screen. At its base were painted panels showing the figures of saints. Their bodies were still intact but their faces had been savagely attacked with some sharp, pointed device, and yet there had obviously been something peremptory about these attacks, and in a couple of cases only the eyes had been scratched out, so that you couldn't see the saint looking back at you.

'See what happens if you leave your churches unlocked,' Kelly said drily.

'I don't get it,' said Dexter. 'Is it vandals?'

'Sort of. But we know the name of the chief vandal,' Kelly said. 'William Dowsing. A Puritan. An iconoclast. He and his men swept through East Anglia destroying graven images wherever they found them, and they found them just about everywhere. Stained glass, carved angels, paintings, brasses, the lot; anything with an image – it all had to go.'

'When was this?' Dexter asked. 'Recently?'

'April sixteen sixty-three. The Reformation. You remember the Reformation, right?'

'Right,' he said, but he sounded unconvincing. Kelly took it as an example of American indifference to what went on in England.

'Dowsing kept a diary,' Kelly went on. 'He enjoyed his work, took pride in it. He listed everything he destroyed.'

'Religion, huh,' said Dexter.

'Dowsing was in his forties,' said Kelly. 'You always think of religious zealots as being substantial and ancient with long white beards, but my guess is that most of his men were more like football fans than men of God: young, stupid, too much testosterone.'

On the south wall of the nave there was a length of red curtain and a cord for pulling it back. Kelly slowly operated the cord and the curtain opened to reveal a mural, a medieval painting of the Day of Judgment. The colours were faded to pale terracotta and powder blue, yet it was still clear and detailed. At the top was a depiction of heaven with the holy trinity in residence. There was Saint Peter at the gate acting as a kind of divine bouncer.

'It's what we English call a doom painting,' Kelly said.

Her favourite characters were four souls hoping to be allowed in the gates. They were naked, very white: three men and one woman, distinguished and defined by their head gear; a king and a queen, a bishop and a cardinal. Each had a little round pot belly. They looked vulnerable and fearful but they seemed to be doing rather better for themselves than the poor souls elsewhere in the painting, who were no less naked but were writhing in agony and falling into the jaws of hell where devils and monsters were ready to torture them with tongs, spears and flame.

Dexter looked at the painting for a long time and he appeared to be fascinated by it. He moved from one spot to another staring into the faces of the saints and devils. Finally he took a couple of limping steps back and said, 'It's fantastic.'

'Yes,' Kelly agreed. 'The story is that when the vicar of the church heard that William Dowsing was on his way he whitewashed over the painting so it wouldn't be destroyed. But something went wrong. The vicar died or went away, and everybody seems to have forgotten that the doom was ever there. For the next two hundred and fifty years people kept painting over it. And then in the late nineteenth century somebody chipped away a bit of paint and found it was still there. It was quite a restoration job to get the paint off and leave the doom intact.'

Dexter continued to give the painting his full attention, and finally he said, 'And have you noticed, the souls who are in hell have genitalia while the ones who've been saved don't?'

Kelly smiled. It was one of the first things she'd ever

spotted in the painting, and although she felt this ought to be a hideous demonstration of the hypocrisy and repressive nature of religion, in fact she found it rather touching.

'And what do you think the artist is trying to tell us?' she said archly.

Dexter laughed. Kelly felt she'd made some sort of a breakthrough. After they'd looked at the rest of the church she drove Dexter back to the Phoenix Inn. She couldn't pretend anything very much had changed. Conversation didn't suddenly flow, and Dexter insisted on hearing the Bach tape again, yet she felt a lot more comfortable. The man had proved that he had at least some small vestiges of soul. She didn't think this was enough to guarantee that the second day was going to be wholly easier than the first, but at least she no longer felt compelled to abandon the arrangement. Dexter asked her if she wanted to come in for a drink, but she declined. As they parted he said he wanted to go to Thorpeness the following day.

MY FAVOURITE
PURITAN

by

Christopher Howell

One man more than any other changed the face and condition of the churches of East Anglia. His name was William Dowsing, a local Suffolk man who did well for himself under Puritanism. In 1643 he was appointed as the Earl of Manchester's visitor of churches, and his 'visits' tended to be very memorable. His job was to seek out popish adornments and graven images, and destroy them. His advantages were that he knew the area well, had a firm uncomplicated religious faith and was indefatigable to the point of obsession. He was a true iconoclast.

We see the results of his fastidiousness throughout the area – stained-glass windows reconstituted from broken fragments, blinded saints, the lead shot in the faces of wooden angels, the blank stones where church brasses were once attached. And there is much we can never see – crosses destroyed, tombs dug up, altars lowered, carvings burnt.

Naturally, he did not operate alone. He had a crew of men, or rather, I suspect, boys. One tends to think of religious zealots as grand old men with granite-like convictions, and certainly Dowsing was in his forties, but my guess is that his men were much younger than him, that they were driven by testosterone rather than zeal, and the image I carry with me of iconoclasm is less of religious disciples than of football supporters. Dowsing's religious confidence gave licence to their instincts.

There are days when I find it almost possible to think of Dowsing as a good man, a moral man, someone who set free his demons in a good cause, who released his appetite for destruction in order to combat what he saw as a greater evil. He had an urge for blankness, for purity. He was a hater of fanciness, of corrupt opulence. But there are other days when he just seems to be a philistine, a boot boy, a vandal.

And it occurs to me that the spirit of William Dowsing is always with us; those dark, destructive, indecent but all too human impulses that we tell ourselves are buried so deeply and yet which are so easily relocated. True belief is only one of the things that can help us find them.

And perhaps today true belief is not even necessary. We can destroy ourselves and our works without any recourse to ideology. Someone nicks the lead off the roof, steals the church plate, the developers build sewers through the churchyard. It's just what happens, the natural way of things. Naturally that which lives must die. That which is constructed must crumble. Man's built creations are likely to last much longer than any man, but in the end circumstances conspire to destroy all our works. Even if the vandals and developers don't get us then the elements will.

Some years ago I was in a ramshackle town in the California desert, a decent and honest enough place, cheerful in its way, not especially dirty, not desperately poor. It had a small shopping mall and a motel and a couple of so-so diners.

I was aware, as I often have been in parts of the United States, that the buildings all looked much the same. Form and function didn't match. The supermarket could be mistaken for the car parts warehouse, the karate school looked much like the thrift store; and I realized that this similarity of construction had, first of all, something to do with a similarity of age. All the town was built at

38

pretty much the same time. There was no sign of the blending together of contrasting styles and historical periods. There was no building in the town that was more than twenty years old. Not only that, it appeared that nothing in the town would ever be more than twenty years old. The buildings simply weren't meant to last longer than that. There would never be any point restoring or refurbishing these buildings. When they were done with they would simply be torn down and other, equally insubstantial, buildings put up in their place.

I realized that, as a European, as a professed fan of culture and architecture, I probably ought to find that prospect quite appalling, and yet I didn't. I found it somehow optimistic, confident, liberating. This was not a place with complicated planning regulations, with rival interest groups to be satisfied or appeased. A man might be free here to build and invent much as he wished, and if he failed, it didn't matter. His mistakes would soon be gone. It was no worse than making a sandcastle. The tide of passing time would soon roll in and wash away all his errors.

The town had a church. It looked beautifully simple, partly in imitation of a European church in that it had a steepled tower and expanses of Gothic windows, and yet it still seemed very typical of the area. It appeared to be made of white wooden clapboards, a clean, honest material, but when I inspected more closely I discovered that the clapboards were in fact made of thin aluminium. There was also a plain wooden cross, some fifteen feet high, set in the churchyard, tucked in behind a white picket fence.

And I wondered, perversely perhaps, just what William Dowsing would have made of this town. It was certainly a place of simplicity, if not of absolute blankness and, although he might have objected to the modestly garish motel and gas station signs, it seemed to be a place largely without graven images.

But I had arrived in the town in daylight and as it got dark my impression changed. I had not been observant enough. The simple wooden cross in the churchyard turned out to have neon tubes embedded in its limbs, and at night they were illuminated like a fairground attraction that could be seen for miles around. Personally I found this appealing, even touching, in a tacky sort of way, but I knew that William Dowsing would have been moved to a frenzy of destructiveness. I thought of the thrill he would have experienced from smashing the glass of the neon tubes, a thrill that would surely be not too dissimilar from smashing church windows, but imagine the extra excitement of electricity, of sparks showering down, of gas escaping, perhaps there would even be small explosions and fire. I decided that William Dowsing would have liked this town.

And he would surely have liked other elements of modern architecture. He wouldn't have been too happy with Pugin or William Morris, but he'd have had no argument with van der Rohe or Gropius. He would have appreciated the International Style. He would have understood Brutalism and Minimalism. He would have understood the vogue for industrial grey carpet, for metal shelving and exposed ducting. He would certainly have understood Abstract Expressionism.

Sometimes I envisage sending teams of modern-day William Dowsings to every house in the country, and letting them unleash their iconoclasm on each and every cosy English domestic interior. Down from the walls would come every picture of cute animals and English landscapes, every calendar, every bedroom poster. Down would come the wallpaper. Depictions of flowers, fruit and foliage would be excised from every surface: from plates and cups and saucers, from bowls and mugs and bread bins, from curtains and sofas and cushions and tea towels and counterpanes. All the visual clutter would go: the postcards from relatives, the get-well-soon cards, the amusing biscuit tins showing teddy bears or the Houses of Parliament. Framed family snapshots would be cleared from mantelpieces. Out would go cutesy fridge magnets, the kids' paintings, porcelain dogs, amusing seaside souvenirs, decorative plates, portraits of the queen, even, God knows, depictions of God himself. And, of course, the ultimate thing that would have to go would be televisions. Imagine the thrill an iconoclast like William Dowsing might have had from putting his puritanical boot through a 24-inch television screen.

3

Kelly lived in a tiny converted chapel on the outskirts of a village called Yoxwell. She'd been more than ready to walk out on her last disastrous live-in boyfriend, and when someone told her there was a chapel available to rent cheap she'd hurried along there expecting lofty spaces, high ceilings and huge expanses of stained glass. But the reality had been a plain building not much bigger than a one-bedroomed cottage. The religious faith that had required such tiny premises must have been simple indeed. It could only have accommodated the most minute congregation, and the God that had been worshipped there must have been a strictly meat and potatoes kind of deity.

If there had ever been ecclesiastical fittings or furnishings they were long gone when Kelly arrived. She'd done some things to give the place a renewed faintly churchy feel. She'd bought one or two pieces of old stained glass, and hung them in front of the windows but they'd come from demolished pubs rather than churches. One showed a Victorian cricketer, one showed Shakespeare. She'd also found a couple of garish plaster Virgin Marys and decked them out with fairy lights.

Inside there was just one big room, a continuous space

with a tall narrow window, but an open mezzanine had been constructed halfway up one of the walls to create a bed platform. There had been no room up there for a proper bed, but Kelly's woodwork skills had allowed her to make one *in situ*, created out of reclaimed wood that had once been part of a fishing boat. It was possible to lie on the mattress, on the bed platform and look out of the top of the main window and see the road and houses and people outside. Kelly had discovered you could even do that while having sex if you used the right position.

Kelly had read in an interior decor magazine that 'you can't wreck a wreck', and had used this as her mantra while decorating the chapel. Everything had been painted in garish, clashing, ungodly colours: two walls purple, two walls burnt sienna, window frames in pillar-box red, doors in lime green, the ladder that led up to the bed platform a sunny yellow.

The furniture was strictly from junk shops but she'd sprayed much of it silver and gold, and where the items were still too ugly to look at she'd draped them in swathes of fabric, mostly old velvets and chenille, but there were one or two lengths of fun fur and nylon animal prints.

All the decorating had been done in a flurry of early enthusiasm the month she'd moved in, and everything had looked new and pristine for a short while. It had been impressive enough to feature in a magazine. She'd been roped into it by a friend of a friend who worked on one of those minor interior decor mags for people who dream of living in the country but will never quite get round to doing it. The headline on the article had read, 'Country doesn't mean conventional'.

She'd had reservations about appearing in the magazine at all, but she was quite pleased by what she'd managed to do with such limited resources and the place looked even better in the magazine than it did in life. But the experience hadn't been entirely simple or easy. For one thing, some of the neighbours began treating her as though she was some sort of celebrity, a minor celebrity certainly, but appearing in print put a little distance between them and her, not least because they suddenly assumed she must be rich. The fact that the chapel was so small, the fact that she worked as a taxi driver made no difference to the way she was perceived. To be featured in a crummy magazine set her apart.

Maybe that was what killed her enthusiasm for further work on the chapel. After the initial burst of activity and creativity she had stopped completely and done nothing more. That had been some years ago. The paint, she told herself, now looked interestingly distressed. Damp and decay had reclaimed the ceiling, streaking it with new milky ways of mould.

There were paintings on the walls, a collection that had required an intense though brief scouring of charity shops. The living room and kitchen contained what she called 'bad pet art'; bad art featuring pets, rather than art featuring bad pets. With some it was a matter of technical incompetence, but more often it was a question of subject matter. There were cute puppies, Yorkshire terriers with ribbons in their hair, melancholy spaniels, comical dachshunds.

Upstairs, around the bed platform, was the collection of 'bad sex art', and here the distinction between bad technique and bad subject matter was harder to separate. There were female nudes that had obviously been copied from photographs in girlie magazines; not very well copied since the paintings showed weird lengthening and foreshortening of limbs, and anatomically impossible poses. But just as often the artist had painted from his imagination, and revealed

45

how unfamiliar he was with the subject. One or two paintings showed couples in intense but inexplicit poses, and in these the artist had tried to instil a spiritual dimension. The couples were on beaches, or posed in front of abstract sunsets or just floating in the clouds.

Taking men up there was always a challenge. Some just saw sex and nakedness and that was enough for them. They were tremendously encouraged and felt Kelly must be a bit of a goer, which wasn't entirely untrue. Others sensed there was irony afoot and wondered if perhaps Kelly didn't take sex quite seriously enough, quite as seriously as they did. By the time they'd made it to the bed, however, they weren't usually deterred by a little thing like irony; although there had been at least two who'd run away thinking that Kelly was only interested in getting them up there to take the piss out of them.

A few, a very few, responded exactly the way she wanted them to. They saw that sex was complicated, serious, funny, a matter of technique, passion, untutoredness and hilarity all at once. It had been a long time since a man like that had graced her bed.

Some people came into the chapel and found it a hellish place, a torture chamber of misdirected kitsch. Others found it sort of amusing, a fun house. But neither group understood how anybody could actually live with it all. For Kelly, however, the decoration had now become more or less invisible. She didn't think about it, was hardly even aware of its eccentricity, and that being the case, she had no incentive to change it. She knew this was not the instinct of the true interior designer, for whom change was everything; redefining volumes, creating fresh looks, finding the latest colours and the coolest new accessories. She wondered what her father would have made of all this mess.

The only clearly unironic item on display was a photograph above the fridge. It showed Kelly, aged ten, with her father. They had their arms around each other, golf putters in their hands, and they were standing on a crazy golf course. The colours in the picture had faded and the outlines had lost their sharpness. It seemed a good deal more innocent that anything else in the house.

Sometimes Kelly lay on her bed looking up at the dark, mottled ceiling and wondered exactly how many other ceilings she'd slept under. How many men had been on top of her, covering her while she looked up at the cracked plaster of strange ceilings?

She thought of sex outdoors, on the beach at Walberswick, on a gravestone in Wangford churchyard, on her back looking up at the wide, cold sky and not experiencing lofty intimations, just wondering how many others were out there, feeling alone and unloved, doing the same as her. And when the man rolled over, pulled her on top, and she felt all that openness behind her, all that vacuity, that scope for mayhem and threat and exposure, then she felt infinitely naked, infinitely vulnerable, poised ready for some cosmic stab in the back.

She wanted sex with someone but not with just anyone. Her standards were high, but not impossible to meet. It saddened her to be alone but not as much as sleeping with the wrong person saddened her. There were so many wrong people, wrong in so many terrible and varied ways and, as she lay there in her bed, she felt herself again assessing Dexter, thinking about him as a sexual partner. Perhaps he wasn't so bad after all. She started to get depressed. Surely it was possible to look at men, to meet them, talk to them, spend time with them without weighing them up sexually. The fact that she found it so impossible proved she was too hungry, too desperate. The extent of her needs guaranteed that her needs would not be met. She got out of bed, got ready for the day ahead.

4

Kelly thought of Thorpeness as one of God's weird though not especially wild places; not that God had much to do with it. Thorpeness was a resort village, spitting distance from Aldeburgh on one side, and even closer to the Sizewell nuclear power station on the other. It was one of those purpose-built bits of seaside, but it had no promenade, no boarding houses, no fun fair, no 'kiss me quick' hats, no whelk stalls. It was not that sort of seaside. It was posh, East Anglian, civilized.

'Created in the early part of the century by a man called G. Stewart Ogilvie,' Kelly explained as she drove. Dexter had brought along another tape, Mahler this time, and it played as she spoke, giving her the feeling that she was doing the voice-over for a rather solemn documentary.

'It wasn't that Ogilvie lacked imagination, but he had a dry, limited, English sort of imagination. He didn't want the place to be vulgar. He did create a boating lake, and there's a golf club that thinks very highly of itself, but it's not exactly fun city. What makes it interesting is the weird architecture. Did you ever get *The Prisoner* on telly in America? Well, it's like a watered-down version of that place.'

Dexter had had a spring in his step when she'd picked

him up that morning. He was still limping of course, but it was a jaunty sort of limp. He had bundled himself into Kelly's car, and even though the effort had made him wince, he smiled once he was seated.

'Maybe it's just the nature of the beast,' said Kelly, 'that if you have the means to build a whole new village, you're congenitally unlikely to have the imagination to build a really interesting one.'

She described the buildings of Thorpeness, said they tended to be individual and individualistic, not wild fantasy exactly, but lots of mock-Tudor, mock-medieval, mock-workers' cottages; a great deal of mockery. There was a big crenellated gatehouse, but it was not the gateway to anywhere in particular, simply running between two blocks of flats. She described the miniature triumphal arch which was in fact the entrance to a public park, but the opening was only wide enough to let one person through at a time and it was made of concrete. She described the thatched sentry boxes, the free-standing dovecote, the almshouses, the strangely hideous church.

'It has the feeling of an eccentric but slightly dour architectural movie set,' she said.

This was actually a quotation from one of her father's books. Inevitably it was her father who had first brought her here, but she came back often and, as with the doom painting in Dunstan, she judged people by their reactions to it. She had hopes for Dexter.

'It does have two genuine tourist attractions,' she said. 'You could argue that neither of them is strictly speaking a folly. They're not quite what they seem, but they're quite useful I suppose.

'There's a nineteenth-century windmill, real enough but nothing was ever ground in it, at least not in Thorpeness.

Ogilvie bought a redundant mill and moved it here, to pump water out of the ground. But having got this water he needed somewhere to put it, so he built a gigantic water tank; that's the other folly, six storeys built up around the tank. The top two look like a small cottage, with a pitched roof, bay window and chimney, perched on top of a narrow, four-storey tower. There are windows on every level, and it's now converted into flats. But the part that looks most habitable, the top two storeys, are actually the water tank. They call it the "House in the Clouds", which I always think is a bit of an overstatement.'

'You're pretty well informed for a taxi driver, aren't you?' Dexter said.

'English taxi drivers always know everything,' she replied, but she should have known he wouldn't accept so blasé an answer.

'I just keep wondering,' he said, 'why a smart young woman like yourself is wasting her life behind the wheel of a cab.'

The combination of flattery and insult was maddening, and it seemed they were back to their relationship of the previous day.

Kelly could only reply, 'I'm not that young.'

'But surely you must have ambitions.'

'Why must I?'

'There's something about you that says you're cut out for more.'

'What kind of something?'

'I don't know. Maybe it's in the genes.'

'There's only the usual stuff in my jeans,' she said, but he didn't get the joke.

'Surely you must want to broaden your horizons, to have an education, to travel, to fulfil your potential.'

51

'If you say I must . . .'

'Perhaps you need a mentor.'

Kelly couldn't tell if he was making a feeble joke or whether, more improbably, he was testing the waters of flirtation. To be on the safe side she said, 'So what subjects would I need mentoring in?'

'All subjects,' he said, and it was still impossible to tell if there was innuendo there.

'Well,' Kelly said, 'yesterday you told me about Bach. So what's it going to be today? Existentialism?'

'Existentialism's pretty straightforward really,' he said, and she couldn't quite believe it when he began to give her a pocket definition of existentialism.

At that moment Kelly felt there was more than enough reason to terminate the arrangement. She thought she could just about tolerate fighting off the boredom of his company, but she was damned if she was going to spend the next few days being mentored.

'What is it that you do with *your* life, Dexter?' she asked as he finished his tutorial.

He looked troubled as though it was a familiar and intractable question.

'You could say I'm a perpetual student,' he said, 'although in fact I only started recently.'

'What do you study?'

'What have you got? Music, literature, a little anthropology, a smattering of history, philosophy. You know the sort of thing.'

Kelly didn't, but she let it pass.

'You're probably thinking I'm a little old to be a student.'

She hadn't been thinking anything of the sort, but now that he mentioned it . . .

'My grandfather was a doctor in LA, made a bundle of

money looking after Industry people. He wanted my father to do the same but Dad was too comfortable or too dumb for college, so he became a realtor, set up his own company, made a whole new bundle of money, still does, and then he wanted me to be in the business with him. And I said fine.

'I went into the family business when I was pretty young. Found I was good at it, in the way that only the young and uncommitted can be good. I made a small bundle of my own, got married. I was *so* good at what I did that by the time I was in my late twenties I was burnt out. So I took some time off. My dad was very understanding. Why wouldn't he be? He's a laidback California kind of guy and I was his best boy. It started out as a one month break, then two months, then six. Then I decided to go back to college, get a real education. I wasn't very smart but I was very committed. I still am.

'And, if you want the full story, that's pretty much why my marriage ended. My wife thought she'd married a business whiz-kid. Turned out she'd married an over-educated slacker.

'So that's what I do – existentially. Whether it's what I am is a different question.'

They arrived in Thorpeness and Kelly parked the car. Perhaps she was letting her mean streak show. She deliberately drove to a far corner of the car park so that Dexter would have to walk that much further on his bad leg. She thought a little bit of physical pain and punishment might be good for him. He did his best to retain his good humour, but when he tried to take her arm to help his progress she pointedly pulled away and walked faster.

'What exactly's wrong with that leg?' she asked.

'I don't really know,' he admitted glumly. 'The doctors call it tendinitis, which means they don't know either. Tendinitis is a condition where—'

53

'It's all right, I don't need that much detail. Are you having treatment?

'A little physiotherapy, some painkillers. Sometimes they pass electric current through it.'

'Has it helped?'

'How can you tell? Who knows how much worse it would be if I hadn't had the treatment? It may get better with time or it may be something I just have to live with. There are good days and bad days.'

'What's today?' she asked.

'Good enough,' he said. 'Better than yesterday.'

'Good.'

So they tramped around Thorpeness. There weren't many people about and Kelly was glad. She found herself embarrassed to be with Dexter. They didn't belong together and she was worried somebody might think they were a pair, or worse, a couple.

Today Dexter had his camera with him and he snapped away at everything he saw. That seemed desperately uncool to Kelly, too touristy, too rubber-necked, and when he asked if he could take her picture she told him not to be so silly. Even Dexter's appreciation of Thorpeness, which seemed genuine, didn't please her. She somehow felt he wasn't enjoying it the right way, the way she did.

'I suppose also,' he said out of thin air, 'that being in your job makes it very difficult for you to have relationships.'

'What?'

'People tend to pair off with partners of a similar social status. Intellectuals marry other intellectuals. Factory girls marry factory boys. But you, I can't see that you'd be very happy married to another taxi driver.'

He happened to be right, but that didn't win him any points with Kelly either.

'Guess I'm still looking for Mr Goodbar,' she sneered.

'Maybe you're looking in the wrong place,' he said.

'Gosh, you know, I think you might be right.'

It was said sarcastically enough but Dexter didn't pick up on that either. He gave her a grand, guileless smile and seemed very happy. It occurred to her that perhaps this was all Dexter really wanted: approval, agreement, someone to say 'how true' after his every utterance. A gloomy silence fell over her.

They struggled up to the windmill and the House in the Clouds, and having looked at them carefully and read the information boards Dexter said he was impressed.

'I really love your English follies,' he said. 'They're so sane, so repressed. In America you have buildings shaped like doughnuts and hot dogs. In Barcelona you have Gaudi. In Vienna you have Hundertwasser. Wild people, creating wild stuff. Here in England a person needs to do so little before he's considered crazy.'

'I suppose you're right,' she said.

'I don't imagine you've ever been to the United States, have you?'

'No,' she said. 'But I've been to Ibiza.'

'"What do they know of England who only England know?" That's a quotation from Kipling.'

'I know.'

'Good.'

And he smiled broadly again and returned to his state of happiness. Kelly couldn't quite believe how easy it had been to work him out. Just agree with him and everything would be fine. She was filled with contempt.

They had lunch at a little snack bar by the boating lake. They ate dull English pies and sandwiches and she felt an urge to apologize for them. Dexter shrugged and said it didn't matter and he exercised some theory about true sophistication meaning that you should eat caviar at the Ritz and dull pies and sandwiches at the snack bar by the boating lake. It was a question of appropriateness. This annoyed her as much as anything Dexter had said so far.

He limped over to the counter and paid for lunch and they went outside. There were a couple of rowing boats on the lake, one containing a vast woman and two small children, the other with a smoochy young couple. Kelly looked at her watch. There was still a lot of day to be got through.

'I bought this,' Dexter said, and he held up a porcelain model of the House in the Clouds. It had been on sale in the snack bar. It was detailed but something in the moulding and varnishing had softened off the hard edges. It was smoother and more streamlined than the real thing.

'Would you carry it for me?' Dexter asked. 'I don't have a pocket big enough.'

This was patently untrue. The model was scarcely more than four inches tall and would have fitted quite easily into the pocket of his jacket.

'What the hell,' Kelly muttered under her breath and took the model from him.

'You know,' Dexter said, 'my knee is feeling a whole lot better. I think I might be able to take a walk along the beach with you.'

'Are you sure?' Kelly asked.

It wasn't that she had developed a concern for his health. She couldn't have cared less whether his leg got better or worse. She was trying to dissuade him because she wanted him to sit on his own and read his book like he had the day before and then she'd be able to walk along the beach by herself. Even as she formulated the idea, she knew she was being unfair. She recognized that if she was taking the man's money she ought at least to be prepared to tolerate his company; but she was feeling selfish and ungenerous.

'Really,' he said. 'I think the exercise might do me good.'

Kelly didn't pretend to be pleased at the prospect but neither did she quite have the nerve to tell him to stay where he was. Slowly they made progress along the shingle beach. It took a certain extra effort to push forward over the rough terrain but Dexter did his best to keep up with Kelly as she set the pace.

Parallel to the beach, set back behind a run of low dunes, was a row of bungalows. No two were the same, yet they all shared a look and a spirit. There was something provisional and impermanent about them. They were more than mere shacks and they were clearly well looked after, yet they lacked the solidity of 'real' houses. There was something capricious about them. They spoke in a curiously dated way of holidays and parties and picnics. They had glass porches and shingle gardens that sprouted poppies or sea holly as well as old anchors and chimney pots and improvised sculpture made out of driftwood.

Most of the bungalows didn't look lived in. They were locked up tightly to keep out the world and the sea. The only sign of life was at a distant blue and white bungalow a long way up the beach. There were a couple of cars parked in front of it and half a dozen people were sitting or standing around the steps and veranda.

By then Kelly had managed to put a certain distance between herself and Dexter. He didn't call after her to ask her to slow down but she decided she'd walk as far as the inhabited bungalow and then stop and wait for him to catch up. As she got closer she could see and hear that the people sitting around were young, loud, probably drunk, five men, one woman. She immediately thought they looked like trouble but it didn't bother her since she intended to give them a wide berth. But when she drew level with the bungalow and sat down on a dune at what she thought was a safe distance, she heard one of the men calling to her.

'Hey, down there! Hey, you!'

She half turned round, not looking at the man doing the shouting, but half a turn was enough.

'It *is* you,' he called. 'Kelly. How the hell are you?'

She turned fully now and looked at the owner of the voice. He was young, big boned, big jawed, dressed in cords and a rugby shirt.

'I may have been a lousy lay,' he shouted, 'but don't say you've forgotten me completely.'

And then it clicked. Oh God. One of her mistakes. The briefest of one-night stands after a New Year's party in Ipswich. She'd been drunk and accepted a lift home with him and when it came to the crunch she couldn't be bothered to fight him off. His name was Peter, she seemed to remember, some sort of farmer, or more likely the son of a farmer; sturdy, earthbound, bullishly dull. But he hadn't been a lousy lay at all. There had been something direct, possibly agricultural, about the way he fucked. It lacked finesse but it was very efficient, very passionate. The passion might not have been long-lived, in fact it had worn off before the alcohol did, but that didn't make it contemptible. Brief localized passion was a tiny, important reminder of something greater, a trailer for the main attraction. Nevertheless, she was absolutely certain she didn't want to repeat the experience with Peter, would have been happy never to see him again, and certainly didn't want a shouted conversation about sex in front of his friends.

'Hello, Peter,' she called back.

'Come and have a drink.'

'I'm with someone.'

'Are you really?'

Kelly pointed down the beach to where Dexter was making slow but determined progress.

'We welcome cripples too,' Peter said, and a couple of his friends laughed.

She could see Dexter watching her, seeing her talk to this stranger and she thought he wouldn't welcome it, and perhaps that in itself was why she accepted the invitation; just to annoy him. She walked over to the bungalow. The little group looked like they'd been drinking for a long time. Peter offered her whisky, gin, Pimm's, beer, wine, but she asked for an orange juice and explained that she was working.

'Kelly's an escort girl,' Peter said to the others. 'She takes it very seriously.'

There was more laughter and Kelly said, 'Oh fuck off, Peter,' and he bowed his head in a gesture of mock submission.

'This isn't your bungalow, is it?' she asked him.

'No. Gerald here's rented it for a couple of weeks.'

Peter indicated which of his friends was Gerald but otherwise made no introductions. The woman, a plump, flashy young thing, seemed particularly hostile towards Kelly's arrival. Gerald was deep in conversation, or at least he was deeply involved in listening to the sound of his own voice.

'In a perfect world this whole area could be the California of England,' he was saying. 'There are lots of people who are into alternative lifestyles, organic farmers, artists, craftsmen. There's a chap up near Beccles who still makes geodesic domes.'

Kelly glared at him, hoping to convey what an idiot she thought he was, but it did no good. She continued glaring and he continued talking, and eventually she stopped glaring in case he got the idea she fancied him.

Dexter arrived at the bungalow, and Kelly hoped that, if nothing else, he might be able to insist that Suffolk wasn't remotely like California. He was looking pained but composed. However, Kelly's instincts about him had been wrong. He was happy to meet some people. He introduced himself and before long he was drinking with them and performing male bonding rituals that crossed the nationality gap and were completely incomprehensible to Kelly. She remembered his hip flask and thought perhaps it was only a shared interest in booze that brought them together. Dexter immediately proved himself to be a fierce and capable drinker and that impressed the others.

Kelly kept herself some distance away from the group, feigning an interest in the weeds pushing up through the shingle, but before long she could hear that she was being discussed again.

'Kelly's been showing me the sights,' Dexter said. 'She's pretty good at it, though I figure she thinks it's beneath her. As a matter of fact, I happen to agree with her.'

Peter agreed too, speaking of her as though he was some old friend who'd given a lot of thought to her talents and career prospects.

'Well, she *is* the daughter of a famous father,' Peter said.

Kelly was surprised to hear him say that. How did he know? She must have been drunker than she remembered when she slept with him. Normally she only talked about her father when she was feeling particularly safe and secure. She listened as Peter proceeded to give a brief, somewhat garbled account of her father's life. Inaccurate though it was, it appeared to be enough to intrigue Dexter. She thought he was looking at her differently, as though she was suddenly

60

more worthy of his respect and attention. She was furious. She left the bungalow and the stupid drinkers and walked away, down to the sea.

When she got there she looked at the pebbles. She still paid homage to the Suffolk tradition of collecting stones that had holes through them, threading them together and hanging them outside the front door to keep witches away. When she was a child she could look forever and not find one. Her father always found them instantly. He had a good eye for that as well as for everything else. He used to tell her she didn't need to keep the witches away, that perhaps she was a witch herself. At the time she'd thought it was a very odd thing for him to say, and she didn't find it much less odd even now.

There were still days when she could comb the whole beach and not find a single pierced stone, but that afternoon she came across two or three before she got as far as the water's edge. She was there a good long time before anyone came after her, and when at last she felt someone's presence beside her, it was Dexter. He had got quite drunk quite quickly and he was holding out a glass.

'Peace offering,' he said.

She took the glass from him and asked, 'What's in it?'

'Just orange juice,' he said.

Kelly sniffed the drink. Whatever it was, it was more than orange juice. She could smell a strong whiff of alcohol coming through. The drink had been spiked. What kind of dim bimbo did he think she was? It was the last straw.

'You're a real charmer, aren't you, Dexter?' she said, and she stormed off along the beach.

She knew there was no way he was going to be able to catch up with her and she didn't turn round and look back until she was at the car park. By then there was no sign of

Dexter. No doubt he had gone back to his drinking pals. Kelly thought they all deserved each other. She got in her car and drove away.

Only when she got home did she realize she was still carrying the model of the House in the Clouds that Dexter had bought. She thought of smashing it but decided that would be childish. Instead she took it into her garden and placed it on the bird table so that visiting birds could knock it over and shit on it.

A PLACE APART

by

Christopher Howell

At eleven o'clock one morning I had a phone call from my girlfriend. She'd recently moved to a new area of London and needed to get her car serviced. Having no regular garage she'd looked in Yellow Pages, found a place nearby and made an appointment. She'd driven there and discovered it was behind a council estate, next to a scrap yard and a shelter for drunks – close to the end of the world by her account – and there in a funky but falling down metal shed were three young, dangerous-looking guys covered in grease, and an even more dangerous-looking older man who was the boss.

She said it was the scariest place she'd ever been; she felt it was a place where a woman could get raped, mutilated, murdered and the body never found; and everybody would say, well, what else would you expect going to a terrible place like that all alone? Having got so far, however, she felt she had to leave the car with them, and she'd been told to come back at the end of the day to collect it. By the end of the day it would be dark and the place scarier still. There was no way she could bring herself to go back there, would I pick the car up for her?

I asked whether the men had said or done anything threatening and in reality they hadn't. They'd actually been perfectly polite; but that wasn't the point, my girfriend insisted, it was just the feel of the place.

I told her with a certain glee that what we were talking about here was gendered space. I said there were male and female environments, designed, more or less deliberately, to alienate members of the opposite sex.

Inevitably there are rather more male versions of these spaces than there are female: they include a great many pubs and clubs, lots of caffs, pool halls, betting shops, football grounds, builders' merchants, courts of law, the Houses of Parliament, prisons, public schools and so on.

But certainly women have some of their own. We've all seen the discomfort that comes over a man who's forced to stand around in a clothes shop while his wife tries on new outfits. Other such spaces include ladies' hairdressers, the older sort of department store, tea shops, wool shops, children's nurseries, and so forth. Interestingly enough, in any culture that creates harems, they too become female preserves from which men, other than eunuchs, are strictly excluded.

I am aware, of course, that spaces may be gendered more specifically than in simple male and female terms. They may display sexual preferences; they may be gay spaces or bisexual spaces or polymorphously perverse spaces. Undoubtedly there are spaces which speak of sexual confusion, sexual repression or sexual blankness.

There are also, increasingly, one or two places which consciously create an atmosphere where men and women can feel equally accommodated. The much reviled English 'wine bar' is surely a triumph of this form; a place where women can feel relatively safe, safer than in a pub or a bar for instance, and where men don't have to feel entirely castrated. Certain unisex clothes shops attempt the same thing, as do some, but by no means all, offices. So do the more general bookshops and record shops, although the more specialist they are the more male they tend to become. More often than not this lack of sexual differentiation

64

seems to be done in the name of commerce rather than political equality. By making spaces attractive to both sexes you can surely double the number of potential customers.

I began to wonder about simple domestic spaces. It seems to me that the home is a place where men and women ought to be able to live together on equal terms, and should therefore be neither specifically male or female. Many men find themselves living in gendered spaces, female spaces in which they don't belong. They live as strangers in their own home, in an environment they didn't choose or create; and some men seem to resent this, or at least pretend an indifference to matters of home furnishing or home comfort. But I suspect this is often a pose. A lot of men actually *want* their homes to be feminized; they crave that old-fashioned phantom, the woman's touch.

I think there is some nonsense talked by architectural theorists about the maleness and femaleness of buildings, as though it was a simple matter of anatomy; as though all towers are phallic and therefore male, or that all vestibules are womb-like and therefore female. It is obvious that a tower may in reality appear quite feminine, that a vestibule may be consciously masculine. We conceive of Paris as a female city, New York as a male one, although I suspect we may be guilty of kneejerk sexism here; romance is considered female, skyscrapers are read as masculine.

And yet there is a simple, undeniable proposition that most architects are male, as are most of their clients, their builders and the planners and lawyers with whom they have to deal; and it seems simple common sense to believe that if buildings and cities were built by women they would be softer, safer, more hospitable places. Certainly, I cannot imagine the woman who would have conceived of, much less created, a place that was as harsh and as alienating as the New York subway, or London's Ronan Point flats or, for that matter, as the garage to which I went at the end of the day to collect my girlfriend's car.

My first reaction was to find the place every bit as intimidating as she had. It was dark, cold, metallic. The floor was concrete, pierced with grave-like inspection pits. There was no natural light inside and the roof was patched with slabs of flaking asbestos. I did not belong there. The mere fact that I wasn't covered in dirt and grease made me feel effete and unmanly. This was not an entirely unfamiliar experience. This sort of male space was designed not only to intimidate and exclude women, but also to exclude men of the wrong tribe; the kind of milksops who can't do their own car servicing, for example. But I was determined not to buy in to this ideology.

I had my camera with me, as I often do, and perhaps because I wanted to provoke a reaction, perhaps because I wanted to alienate myself still further from the tribe of mechanics who worked there, I started taking photographs of the garage. I expected to be laughed at, to be abused, to be told that I was mad. But the guys looked at me and seemed more or less indifferent to my activity until one of them, being waggish no doubt, but without being simply or entirely sarcastic, came up to me and said, 'It's not much but we call it home.'

5

Kelly knew that her father wasn't always right about everything. For instance, the local garage where she had her own car serviced and repaired was a clean, orderly, unthreatening place run by a couple of quiet, respectful middle-aged brothers who treated her with greater deference than she thought was her due. There were other things she didn't like about that essay: the mention of this 'girlfriend'. Who *was* that? Some air-headed floozy? Some media tart? What was her father doing running around taking care of this stranger's emotional and automotive needs when he had a wife and daughter in Suffolk who were far more in need of him? She'd tried to get her mother to share the same sense of outrage and betrayal, but in this, as in much else, her mother had been a disappointment to her.

Kelly felt her mother should be something other, something more. She had once been a sort of hippie; not the wild, drug-taking, marching on the Pentagon type of hippie, more the wide-hipped, earthy, nurturing sort, and perhaps it wasn't such a big leap from being that to becoming the good home-maker she now professed to be, but still it depressed Kelly. Her mother lived a cosy, quiet, uneventful life in a neat little nineteen-seventies semi-detached house that her father would not have been seen dead in, but the house had come later, after his death, along with a second husband.

After Christopher Howell died Kelly's mother got remarried, to a man called George. He was an honest man, a decent man, possibly even a good man, but he was also, in Kelly's intense, unfair opinion, a very, very boring man. He worked for a company that sold heavy agricultural equipment, but his part in it simply involved shuffling figures and pieces of paper in an office in Norwich.

No doubt it had been quite brave of him to take on a widow with a teenage daughter as difficult as Kelly, and he'd tried hard to make friends with her and had been quite philosophical when she refused to have anything to do with him. He even helped pay some of the rent on the bedsit she moved into when she was seventeen, although no doubt his motives for helping her leave home weren't entirely altruistic.

Even then Kelly could see that George made her mother happy, although at that point in her life she didn't much care about her mother's happiness. But George went and died too. It was sudden but not unpredictable. He was a fat, slow-moving man with high blood pressure, a bad diet and a job he found stressful. He keeled over one humid August afternoon in the car park outside his office and was dead before the ambulance arrived.

When Kelly looked back she was amazed by her own selfishness, by how little sympathy she'd felt for her mother, how little grief for George. Her mother took his death to be the end of something, perhaps the end of trying. She'd been married to a risky, difficult, interesting man, then she'd been married to a safe, secure, boring man, and it had all come to the same thing. Everything had been taken away, twice.

She would make sure that nothing would ever be taken from her again.

George had found Kelly's mother beguilingly different. By his standards she was arty and extravagant, a Bohemian. She was a splash of colour in his subdued, toned-down life. Once he was gone, she lost much of her colour too. She stopped being extravagant, stopped being arty. She became determined to lead a life that was thoroughly ordered, thoroughly controlled. She did her very best to become a boring, well-behaved, suburban widow, with some success.

She lived on a quiet, well-groomed little estate just fifteen miles down the road from Kelly. Fifteen miles wasn't quite far enough away, but there were times when a million miles wouldn't have been enough.

Kelly teased her mother about the mundanity of the house, and as with all teasing there was something important at stake. She told her that the widow of 'the greatest modern English architect never to have built a building' should live in quirkier, more subversive style; in a folly tower or a Gothic gate lodge or a converted fire station, something like that. Kelly felt there should be eccentric paintings and sculpture everywhere, *trompe l'œil* features at every turn, outlandish decor, wacky furniture.

Her mother pointed out that she had bought the house years after her father died, partly with the insurance money George's death had given her. Christopher Howell had nothing to do with her current life, and even if this had been the house they'd lived in together, she still wouldn't have wanted to turn it into a museum to him.

In fact the house wasn't entirely devoid of Christopher Howell. There were a couple of curious, scrappy architectural drawings displayed in the hall. One showed a building in the shape of a back scratcher, a tall, spindly tower that ended in the five extended digits of a stylized hand. The scale of the drawing was exaggerated so that the building reached up from a patch of bare wilderness, way up into a vast sky so that the tips of the fingers were surrounded by clouds. The other picture was a series of rough sketches of pyramid-shaped buildings, some on stilts, some resting on the ground or on water, some just floating in space. Little domestic touches had been added to each of the pyramids, a television aerial, a porch, a dormer window, a two-car garage.

The drawings looked out of place among the overstuffed sofas and swagged floral curtains and cheap but tasteful antiques that filled the rest of the house. They looked even stranger given that the other paintings on the walls were careful, softly coloured East Anglian landscapes and sea-scapes. The local ladies who visited the house these days probably thought the Howell drawings were a bit of an eyesore but they would be too polite to say so, and Kelly's mother never apologized or explained.

They should have seen the walls when her father lived in Kennington, in London. It was a moment when Christopher Howell's skills at finding, or getting others to find, elegant places for him to live had failed and he'd had to move into a grotty little bedsit behind the cricket ground. He never complained and Kelly was too young to fully understand his discomfort, but inevitably he didn't take his young daughter to bedsitland with quite the same panache as he would have taken her to some eighteenth-century cottage or Barbican penthouse. But to Kelly the place had still seemed wonderful.

She couldn't imagine quite what the room must have been like to start with. It was her experience that nasty rented accommodation always had especially nasty, patterned wall-paper. Here the walls were white, but she thought it was quite possible her father had painted them himself. Whatever the origins of the white surfaces, her father had seen them as a blank canvas.

He told her he'd started to doodle on the wall beside the bed, a doodle he'd immediately seen as a sort of road map showing a long broad thoroughfare with many junctions and side streets. But then the doodle began to have a life of its own. That first main street led to other roads, to round-abouts, dual carriageways, motorway flyovers and tunnels, and he'd drawn all these in. This had led to the creation of rivers, railways, canals. The map had spread from one wall to two, to three to four, and it had risen up to the ceiling where the separate wall maps had converged around the ceiling rose. From certain angles it resembled an elaborate spider's web.

He hadn't drawn every single building in detail but he'd sketched in symbols that might be looked at as strange ground plans: a cinema shaped like a movie camera, a school in the shape of a saxophone, a swimming pool shaped like a brain, a drive-in restaurant in the shape of a coffin. Her father's tastes did not run to the whimsical and although he had created an imaginary kingdom, there was nothing fey or childlike about it. There was a suicide bridge, and an area of open space called 'Killing Fields'.

Then there were some dark jokes: nuclear reactors pos-itioned next to hospitals, prisons for sex offenders that over-looked girls' schools. There were housing developments that encircled toxic waste sites. And he had shaded in the ceiling rose so that it looked like a volcano which threatened to erupt and destroy the whole kingdom. Kelly loved it. Her father had asked her if she wanted to help colour it in but she preferred it in black and white.

Her father didn't stay in that room very long, moving on rapidly to a much more stylish, borrowed houseboat. Kelly

71

always wondered how the landlord had reacted to the redecoration. She supposed he was furious and had had the wall repainted. She imagined it took a good few coats. That might be a fruitful area for some particularly dedicated Christopher Howell scholar. He or she could track down the bedsit, find some process by which the covering layer of paint could be removed and reveal the Christopher Howell drawing underneath.

When Kelly got home from her father's bedsit she'd tried a similar sort of thing in her own bedroom. She started drawing a city on the wall above the radiator. She'd got as far as creating a dam, a monorail station and a ring road before her mother discovered her and gave her a good slapping. It was one of the first things she'd never been able to forgive her mother for.

Kelly had been planning a visit to her mother for a while now. Enough time had elapsed since the last one for guilt and daughterly duty to reconvene. The promise of a week's work from Dexter had made her postpone her plans, but now, having ditched him, she had an unexpected free day and she felt she might as well get the visit over with.

She didn't believe she'd really seen the last of Dexter since, if nothing else, she intended to confront him and extract two days' wages; but she decided that could wait. She switched on the answerphone and got on with her day. She would visit the gym and then go to her mother's.

The gym was nearly empty, just a few retired male narcissists and herself. She rowed, did some weights, then ran a couple of miles on the treadmill, stopping before it came to feel too symbolic. Exercise gave her no great pleasure but she knew it must be doing her some good. And even if her body wasn't toned and hard, she took some comfort in thinking (as with Dexter's leg) that it would all be so much worse if she didn't give it the treatment. When she'd finished she showered and came out feeling just about strong enough to cope with her mother.

It was to be an unannounced visit. It worked better that way. If she told her mother a day or two in advance that she was coming, then she'd spend the intervening days preparing for the visit, specifically preparing food. Kelly couldn't remember exactly when her mother had started expressing maternal feeling through hard work in the kitchen but it was now an unshakeable pattern. There'd be cakes and pastries and pies, and Kelly would be expected to eat most of this on the spot while her mother watched. If she ate everything her mother thought she should, then she would be considered a good girl and earn motherly approval. If she ate less than that, she was being a bad girl, a bad daughter and therefore undeserving of parental love. By arriving unannounced she hoped it might be a day when her mother was less prepared.

It was late morning when she got to the house. She pulled up outside and entered by the back door, without knocking. She could hear the television blaring in the living room, but as she called out 'Hello' her mother immediately turned the set off, and by the time Kelly sauntered into the room her mother was on her feet, a duster in her hand, pretending to be in the middle of vital housework. There were times when Kelly felt bad about the effect she had on her mother, but not today. Today she was feeling tough.

'Not working?' her mother said by way of hello.

'Not as hard as you, obviously,' Kelly replied.

'It's all right for some people.'

'Yes, it *is* all right,' Kelly said. 'It's all right for people to do something other than work, especially if they're self-employed like me.'

73

'I thought you'd have thrown that old leopardskin jacket away by now,' her mother said.

'Not until you knit me a new one.'

'It's not very attractive, is it?'

'I'm only trying to attract lovers of fake fur.'

'I wouldn't have thought you could afford to be so choosy.'

And so on. It happened every time. Kelly always went to her mother's with the best of intentions and the moment she got in the door she felt the years being stripped away from her until she had regressed and turned into a sulky, difficult fifteen-year-old. Her mother always went right along with the act, played the neurotic parent of the neurotic adolescent. But now there was the added problem of Kelly being left 'on the shelf'. For all that her mother wanted to protect herself from ever being involved with anybody again, she still wanted her daughter to be safely attached to someone. It didn't have to be marriage, it didn't have to be dull, but she wanted her daughter to have a love life. Kelly thought that from her mother's point of view it must be like watching a stunt woman. She liked the vicarious thrill of seeing someone else risk their neck.

'Well, I don't know what I'm going to give you to eat,' Kelly's mother said. 'It's bad of you not to let me know when you're coming.'

'It was a spontaneous decision. You remember spontaneity, eh, Mother?'

'I'll just have to have a look in the freezer, but don't expect much.'

'I don't want much.'

'Well, you certainly need something. Bad diet always shows in the face.'

And so on. Kelly had heard there were mothers and daughters in the world who had real conversations and related to each other like real human beings, even talked to each other about things that mattered, but nothing in her own background had ever persuaded her that this was anything other than improbable science fiction.

They were about to get into a seriously petty argument about diet and health and complexion when there was a knock at the kitchen door. Kelly's mother was the sort of person whose life did not accommodate unexpected arrivals. Kelly's own visit was shocking enough, but a second visitor obviously spelled disaster. She looked at Kelly as though this new arrival was all her fault too, and as she went through to answer the door she looked briskly about her as if thinking of arming herself with a bread knife or rolling pin.

Kelly sat down on the floral, overstuffed, living-room sofa. She heard the kitchen door open and she could hear a conversation taking place, a man's voice, though she couldn't make out any of the words. Finally, she heard her mother say in an unnecessarily loud, clear voice, 'In that case you'd better come in,' and she returned to the living room trailed by Dexter. He was carrying a huge bundle of pink and white carnations, and with a flourish he presented them to Kelly.

She looked scornfully at him, dismissively at the flowers. She took them without saying thank you, without saying anything at all, and immediately handed them on to her mother. Despite herself, her mother was beaming. She didn't like her life to be disrupted by strange arrivals, but if the stranger was a foreign man bearing flowers, well, that had an appeal to it. The fact that Kelly had never mentioned any such man, the fact that the flowers were now with her rather than with her undeserving, unappreciative daughter, added to her enjoyment.

'You've got some nerve coming here,' Kelly said, and only then did she take a good look at Dexter's face. The flowers

75

had been a distraction, probably a deliberate one. She saw now that he had a huge, fresh, curdling black eye.

'I've come to apologize,' he said. 'I behaved pretty badly.'

Kelly's mother's eyes widened in anticipation of hearing something really good and juicy.

'He spiked my drink,' Kelly explained to her, hoping that would make her mother disapprove of Dexter. No such luck.

Her mother tutted. 'Well really, Kelly, I don't think that's so terrible.'

'If I hadn't noticed, if I'd taken the drink and then driven the car, if I'd been stopped by the police—'

'That's a lot of ifs,' her mother said.

'No, Kelly's right,' said Dexter. 'It was pretty bad of me. I behaved like a, I don't know what the word is . . . a cad.'

Kelly's mother was doubly thrilled and encouraged to hear that there was such a thing as caddishness still left in the world.

'In any case, Kelly,' she said, 'if Dexter's big enough to apologize then I think you have to be big enough to accept that apology.' And without changing her tone of voice she added, 'Will you stay and have some lunch with us, Mr Dexter?'

'That's very kind of you but I don't want to impose.'

'You won't be imposing.'

'Well, only if it's all right with Kelly.'

'Since when did I have a say in anything?' Kelly said in her best moody adolescent's voice.

They moved to the kitchen and Kelly's mother began assembling the ingredients of an unnecessarily lavish lunch.

'It's no trouble at all,' she said for Dexter's benefit. 'I don't get nearly as much company as I'd like.'

Kelly sat down at the kitchen table, and Dexter immediately planted himself next to her, causing her to stand up and find the view of the garden very interesting.

'How did you find me here?' she hissed.

'I asked around,' said Dexter. 'It's a small world. You and your mother are quite well known. It took a little work, but I was very motivated to see you and apologize.'

She supposed that had to be true. He had apparently gone to some trouble. It would have been nice to attribute his presence to genuine regret and belated chivalry, and her mother appeared happy to do so, but Kelly needed more convincing.

'How did you get the black eye?' she asked.

'Really, Kelly,' her mother said, as if black eyes were something embarrassing like a birthmark or a hare lip that polite people didn't refer to in conversation.

'I got it from your friend Peter, as a matter of fact.'

'He hit you?'

'We hit each other. I think I probably hit him harder than he hit me, but it was a close thing. I'm sure he has a black eye too.'

'How old are you?' Kelly demanded.

He was puzzled, didn't understand her question.

'Isn't it time you grew up?' she added.

'I hit him because he said something very tacky and wouldn't take it back.'

'Well, show me your duelling scar,' Kelly snapped.

'If it makes any difference, he actually said something very tacky about you.'

'It makes no difference at all,' she said, but she knew that wasn't strictly true.

'Look, there was a problem and I did my best to fix it, OK?'

'Oh please,' she said, and a part of her did indeed think that Dexter and Peter were a couple of stupid schoolboys who couldn't be trusted to hold their drink and behave decently. At the same time, she certainly wasn't displeased that Peter had been hit, and despite all her finer feelings, despite what she knew about the evils of male violence, there was something deep in her hormones, swirling around in the silt of her race memory, that went alarmingly warm and gooey at the idea of men fighting over her.

'So, what did the bastard say?' Kelly asked.

'I don't want to repeat it,' said Dexter. 'No way could I repeat it while I'm a guest in your mother's house.'

'Thank you, Dexter,' said Kelly's mother.

The kitchen table was filling up with lunch: slabs of meat, cheese, pâté and pork pies, bowls of salad and fruit, different kinds of bread and crackers, a tureen of soup, some olives, pickled onions, chutneys. Dexter made manly noises of approval.

All through lunch he was the perfect guest. He explained to Kelly's mother about his bad leg and why he was employing Kelly, and he did it all with a grace that Kelly hadn't seen before. Her mother was charmed. At times he almost seemed to be flirting with her. Being good with mothers was not a trait Kelly much valued in men, nevertheless she could see that her mother's approval of Dexter was spreading into a more general, if no doubt very temporary, approval of her daughter. Meanwhile her mother was showing great concern over Dexter's black eye, even offering him a piece of raw steak for it.

'It's nothing much,' he said.

'Coming all the way to England with a damaged knee, that's very brave, very determined of you,' she said.

Dexter smiled weakly and shrugged.

'The truth is, I'm in England with a damaged heart. That pains me a lot more than my knee does.'

For one glorious moment Kelly wondered whether he was sending her mother up something rotten, that at some point he'd turn to Kelly, drop the act and burst out laughing. But no, there was no obvious irony there. He might have been putting on an act but it was an act he apparently believed in.

'Well look, Dexter,' said Kelly as lunch ended, 'you've apologized, you've been fed, I've accepted your apology. Now, if you just pay me off for the time I worked, we can call it a day.'

Without hesitation Dexter produced his wallet and dealt out a full hand of crackling, machine-fresh notes. He gave Kelly all she was owed and then added another twenty pound note.

'Is that a tip?' Kelly asked.

'If you like.'

'Well, thank you, sir.'

Her mother watched the financial transaction with mild disapproval, as though the exchange of money was again something that didn't take place in the better sort of homes, and then Dexter took even more money from his wallet and tried to give that to Kelly too.

'What's that?' she asked.

'That's today's wages. I'd like to carry on with our arrangement for the rest of the day.'

'I'm not working today, not for you or anybody else.'

'It's not a bad offer, is it? A full day's pay for half a day's work.'

'It's not about money.'

'Look,' Dexter pleaded, 'at the very least I'm going to need to call a cab, and you're going to have to drive yourself home. All I'm asking is that you drop me off on the way.'

'Go on, Kelly,' her mother said. 'You've already spent

more time here than you usually do, I can tell you're itching to go.'

'Thanks a lot, Mother.'

'Oh come on, give the poor man a chance.'

A chance to do what, Kelly wondered, yet she knew she wouldn't win this one. She was all too familiar with her mother's habit of taking any side that was different from hers. She knew she might as well give in now and save herself a lot of grief and time. Besides, she really did want to get out of her mother's house.

'OK, I'll drive you home,' she said, 'but don't pay me. I'm just giving you a lift, all right?'

'We'll see,' he said.

They managed to leave Kelly's mother's house, but only after Dexter had expressed unnecessarily exuberant thanks, offered to do the washing up, and graciously turned down the chance of taking some leftovers with him.

As Kelly accelerated the car away from the house he said, 'What is it with interior decor? At seventeen you tell yourself that when you get a place of your own you'll paint the walls purple and orange, have the ceilings black with silver stars, that you'll carpet it with Astroturf and sit on inflatable sofas. But by the time you get your own place your tastes have settled down and you want something easy to live with.

'Like when my wife moved out, she took a lot of her stuff with her and I thought, This is going to be OK, I'll be a bachelor boy, and I'll have red and black leather furniture, and satin sheets and a classic pinball machine. But then, two weeks later, I wished she was there doing all the stuff that I never even noticed, arranging cushions and buying cut flowers. Or is that just stupid and sexist of me?'

Kelly couldn't be bothered to engage. 'Maybe,' she said.

But Dexter wanted more attention. 'Look,' he said, 'I was

thinking, since we're nearby, whether we might take a look at the nuclear power station. Sizewell? Is that the name?'

'I don't want to take you to Sizewell,' said Kelly.

'Look, I really am sorry that I spiked your drink.'

'Fine. You're sorry. But so what? Forget it. It's over.'

'But I want to explain why I did it.'

'Because you're an arsehole?'

'If you say so, then I guess I am, but I had other reasons too.'

'I don't need to hear this.'

'But I need to tell you. Look, I don't know, I guess it's about wanting to make a good impression on you. Don't laugh. OK, I know I'm not doing so well. I knew you didn't like me very much and I wanted you to like me. I thought if you were more relaxed, if we got drunk together maybe, then things would be easier. OK, I know it sounds stupid now.'

'It sounds a little desperate.'

'Is wanting to be liked a sign of desperation?'

'Sometimes. You didn't seem to be desperate with my mother.'

'I don't suppose I was trying to impress her.'

Feeling manipulated but not entirely unwillingly, Kelly found herself driving in the direction of Sizewell, a tiny fishing village that had been overwhelmed by the arrival of one and then another power station. There was still a beach and a few fishing boats, but there was also a big car park and a picnic area and a café, for the tourists drawn to the threatening weirdness of the place. She pulled the car off the road and into the gravel of the parking area.

'Why do you want to impress me, Dexter?'

'I don't know. I guess because I'm impressed by you,' he said.

81

She was out of the car and halfway to the beach before Dexter had struggled out of his seat. She waited for him at the water's edge and when he arrived they began to walk slowly, gently along the beach. The sun was feeble, the sea was a thick opal green and the power stations stood out hard and sharp-edged.

There was Sizewell A and Sizewell B. The former was a grey, frightening, shabby building, rugged and four-square with stained concrete walls, a death factory. There was scaffolding huddled round one corner. By contrast Sizewell B looked like something constructed out of children's building blocks. From the beach it appeared as a long, low block of shiny blue metal, crowned with a simple, sparkling white dome. It looked cheerful, friendly, totally harmless.

'It doesn't look much like a nuclear power station,' said Dexter.

'No? What should a nuclear power station look like?'

'Like Sizewell A, I guess.'

Kelly smiled as though Dexter had proved some point for her.

'What did your father think of it?' he asked.

'He never saw it. He was dead before Sizewell B was completed.'

'Do you think he'd have liked it?'

It was not an unfamiliar question, in fact it was the kind of question she asked herself all the time. She often looked at the world, at buildings and spaces and environments and then wondered how they would appear through her father's eyes.

'Yes, I think he'd have liked it,' she said. 'He'd have liked the colour, the bold shapes, the apparent simplicity of it. He'd have thought it was a pretty good joke.'

'What's the joke?' Dexter asked.

'The joke is that it looks like a big, safe, friendly building, when in reality it's an atom splitter and if it blows up it takes half of England with it. The half I happen to live in.'

'Does it scare you?'

'Some days, yes.'

'But you still live here. Why don't you go somewhere safer?'

Kelly had no satisfactory answer to that. She'd often thought of moving on, and not only because of the nuclear reactor on her doorstep, but she never had, and she wondered if she ever would.

'I'm not putting you down,' said Dexter. 'Hell, I live on a fault line in California. Why don't I move away?'

'We could go on a tour of the plant,' Kelly said. 'They spend a lot of time telling you how safe it all is.'

'I don't think so,' said Dexter, and she was glad he'd said that, 'but I wouldn't mind checking out the visitors' centre.'

The tide had recently gone out and left its shabby residue along the beach. Up ahead of them, lying diagonally across their path, was a long, black, tattered piece of driftwood, looking like a decayed snake with a sharp, pointed head. They came to it and stopped. Kelly walked round it as though viewing a piece of difficult but intriguing modern sculpture. She looked across at Dexter. She thought he wasn't the sort of man who would understand the attractions of flotsam and jetsam. She wasn't even going to attempt to explain. But then, unbidden, Dexter said, 'It's great. Really great. Do you want to take it home with you?'

She did, very much, but she didn't see how they could. She looked back at how far they'd come from the car park. It was a fair distance. The piece of wood was heavy and awkward, and Dexter, hampered by his bad leg and his walking stick, didn't look like he'd be a great deal of use. Still, she wanted to try.

'You sure you can manage?' she asked.

'Sure. It'll be worth it.'

That was exactly what she thought. They each grabbed an end. The wood was frayed, splintering with dampness and felt even heavier than it appeared.

As they walked back Dexter said, 'My family has a kind of vacation home out in the desert in California. When I was a kid I was always picking up weird bits of stuff, bones, hub caps, cactus skeletons. They thought I was nuts. At the end of each vacation I'd want to take it all home with me. I had to do a lot of arguing. A lot of tears got shed; mostly mine.'

Kelly found herself feeling curiously sympathetic towards her imagined picture of the young boy.

'You know, Dexter,' she said, 'when you don't try to be liked you can be quite likeable.'

They loaded the length of driftwood into the back of Kelly's car. She was surprised by the ease with which Dexter operated. No doubt he was spurred by his determination to impress her, but this time he didn't seem at all desperate.

They drove to the visitors' centre at the power station and went inside. It was all very friendly and multi-media, lots of lights and television screens, and buttons to press. There was a section through a model house showing how power came in and how it was used. There were displays showing how atoms were split. There was a geiger counter and some mildly radioactive materials. None of it entertained them for very long.

'Not a great selection of souvenirs for sale,' said Dexter. 'I was hoping there'd be a model of Sizewell B. It looks so straightforward, so easy to make.'

'It only looks like that from one angle. I know it looks like a single block with a dome on top, but it's really a lot more complex than that. The white dome doesn't actually sit on top of the block at all, it's free standing and it's some way back, and it isn't just a dome, it's a stumpy little tower with a hemispherical roof. And the blue part isn't a simple block at all. If you see it from the air it's very messy.'

'You've seen it from the air?'

'I once went out with a guy who flew. He hired a plane and we went over.'

'They didn't shoot you down?'

'They didn't even try,' said Kelly.

She became aware of Dexter gathering up his forces to say or ask something important. When it came it didn't seem so monumental to her. All he said was, 'Would you come and have a drink with me now?'

'No, not tonight, Dexter.'

'Tomorrow?'

'Maybe tomorrow.'

'And will you come and pick me up in the morning? Does our arrangement still stand? Where are you going to take me?'

'I'll think of something,' said Kelly.

She drove him back to the Phoenix, then went home. On the way she started to wonder if she was strong enough to get the lump of driftwood out of the car without someone's help.

A FORM OF WORDS

by

Christopher Howell

I have been thinking about ergotopoeic buildings. I believe the word is my own invention. If an onomatopoeic word reveals its meaning by its sound, then an ergotopoeic building reveals its meaning by its look. The form of such a building doesn't only show its function, it *advertises* it. It is the very opposite of Robert Venturi's decorated shed. Let me explain.

First we have buildings that have nothing whatsoever to say about themselves or the activities or the people they contain. These are indeed a sort of shed that may be gently differentiated into supermarkets or carpet warehouses or video stores or multiplex cinemas by a little bit of judicious interior design and shop fitting, and by erecting a sign on the front. One day, I suspect, we may learn to love these buildings as much as Venturi apparently does, but I also suspect that for most of us that day is still some way off.

Next there are buildings that are recognizable from familiarity or custom, even though their form doesn't seem to be absolutely necessitated by their content. A certain kind of architectural style has become synonymous with specific usages. I am thinking of art deco cinemas for example. There is no absolute need for them to have fluted towers, curved canopies, to be tiled and so forth, but the existence of these feature aids our ability to identify the building, increases its visibility in the landscape. Similarly banks try to look solid and ancient, good schools and colleges try to look serious and substantial. Some English pubs try to look welcoming and friendly, others try to look fierce and edgy. There are sound business reasons for all this.

Then there are buildings that seem irreducible and unalterable simply because of the function they fulfil and the activity they contain. One cannot, for example, imagine a sports arena that's much different from Wembley Stadium or Yankee Stadium or indeed the Colosseum: a big central arena with lots of surrounding accommodation for spectators. There seems to be no other workable option. Equally, it's impossible to imagine an aeroplane hangar that differs in any very significant way from all the aeroplane hangars we're already familiar with. Greenhouses are always going to look like greenhouses. Nobody needs to reinvent the bus shelter.

This coincidence of form and function strikes us as good and honest, but some buildings, of course, consciously disguise their function. It may be a kind of *trompe l'œil* or it may be a kind of embarrassment, a need for discretion; so Las Vegas casinos are shaped like circus tents or Roman palaces or Chinese pagodas, anything to disguise the fact that these are places where people go to have their money taken away from them. I have seen estate agents' offices shaped like Greek temples, domestic garages that look like Elizabethan cottages. It's hard to feel any great moral outrage at this, and personally I'm more inclined to experience a rather melancholy feeling of bathos, but no doubt there are those who would see these structures as a perversion of what architecture should be.

Then we come to buildings such as Blackpool Tower or the Eiffel Tower: structures that are not without function, but whose chief function is to be eye-catching. We are in the realm of tourist attractions, I suppose, and I would guess that the Snow Queen's Palace at Disneyland is the most extreme and successful of these;

88

there is no snow, no queen and the building is not actually a palace; nevertheless, it serves its purpose ideally as a trademark and place of entertainment. It is not, I think, in the conventional sense of the word a folly since it is precisely functional. True, there's a dislocation between form and function, yet the spectator is not deceived. He knows that he's only looking at a trademark, whereas a spectator seeing Gothic ruins in a piece of Augustan landscaping might possibly believe he was seeing the real thing.

But none of the above structures could possibly qualify as ergotopoeic. So let's compare two Los Angeles landmarks: the Coca-Cola bottling plant and the Capitol Records building. The former looks like a ship, complete with portholes and guard rails and funnel. It is certainly eye-catching, and undoubtedly there is folly in its conception. It is certainly deceptive in that it tries very hard not to look like a manufacturing and bottling plant. But even though it resembles a ship, it isn't trying to deceive anyone into believing that it actually *is* a ship. It's an amusing building. It looks good natured and free spirited. One assumes that working for Coca-Cola isn't all fun and games, but the architectural style is in keeping with the perceived and created image of the product that's bottled inside. But the question one asks about this building's form is 'Why?' What's the point of the Coca-Cola plant looking like a ship? What's the connection between a tooth-rotting soft drink and an ocean liner? The answer is 'none'. And that's why it's not an ergotopoeic building, whereas the Capitol Records building is.

The Capitol building is a tall, layered, cylindrical block with a spike emerging from its flat roof. From many angles and especially from the air, it looks like a stack of vinyl records on a spindle. There's no functional reason why it should look that way, but as a means of self-definition and self-revelation it's unbeatable. Anybody who drives past could reasonably assume it had something to do with the record business. For the Coca-Cola building to compete it should be shaped like a Coca-Cola bottle.

The Americans undoubtedly are rather good at this sort of thing. As we travel through roadside America, and let's face it, all America is roadside America, we see doughnut shops shaped like doughnuts, fruit stalls shaped like gigantic apples or oranges. Historically guitar-playing movie stars have had guitar-shaped swimming pools. Eero Saarinen's TWA terminal at what was Idlewild airport was convincingly birdlike, and I understand there's a turkey farmer in California whose house is shaped just like a giant turkey.

I think this is great. I think there should be a law that says all buildings should be ergotopoeic. All buildings should reveal what goes on inside them simply by the way they look. So, abbatoirs would be made in the shape of beef carcasses. Brothels would be in the shape of breasts or phalluses (I know Ledoux got there first on this one with his House of Sexual Instruction). Public toilets should be in the shape of giant faeces. And nuclear power stations should, of course, be in the shape of giant mushroom clouds.

6

She was woken by the ring of the telephone. She looked at the alarm clock to see it was still ridiculously early, but she answered it nevertheless. She supposed it would be Dexter but she heard her mother's bright, alert voice.

'This is ridiculously early,' Kelly said.

'I wanted to get you before you started work.'

'You've certainly done that, by several hours.'

'Besides, I couldn't wait any longer to hear more about Dexter. You're a sly boots.'

Kelly groaned theatrically. She should have known.

'He seemed very nice,' her mother said.

'Oh sure. He drinks, he gets into fights, he's what every woman dreams of.'

'But you're not every woman, as you so often tell me, and he does have charm.'

'Yes,' Kelly admitted grudgingly, 'he does sometimes have charm.'

'Spending all day together cooped up in your car, it must get quite intimate.'

'Oh come on, Mother.'

'I just want you to know,' and now her mother sounded

91

grimly, achingly sincere, 'that I really hope it works out for you this time.'

'Oh, for God's sake.'

'I know I've made mistakes, Kelly, and I know I haven't always been there for you the way I should have been, but I always did my best, Kelly, and I always wanted the best for you.'

'Oh please, Mother, what is it? Have you been at the Bailey's again, or have you read some new self-help book?'

Her mother was not deterred.

'I realize you don't know this man very well, but that doesn't matter. I could tell there was something between you, call it chemistry if you like. I looked at the two of you sitting at my kitchen table and it made me very happy.'

Kelly stopped protesting. This was so crazy, so inappropriate that there was nothing to do but let it run its course.

'And I'll tell you something else,' her mother said. 'In some strange way he reminds me of your father.'

Two hours later Kelly was in her car, driving Dexter swiftly along the A12. Today's musical appreciation class involved listening to *The Magic Flute*.

'You know,' said Kelly, 'sometimes I think my taste for ruins is as great as my taste for buildings. You can put it all down to my father, of course.'

Kelly drove effortlessly and casually, and felt no further need to talk. There had been a time when her taste for ruins had extended to men. She'd had a string of ruined boyfriends: drinkers, drug takers, petty criminals, major neurotics, the inadequate, the occasionally mad. She had believed that somewhere in the ruined architecture of their being she could make out the blueprint of a standing edifice. She had wanted to believe that with a little help from her these ruins could be refurbished and made whole.

That summer, before she met Dexter, was the first time she'd seriously begun to shed these notions. She had concluded that people were essentially unimprovable. A little bit of redecoration and smartening up might just about be possible, but not much more. If men weren't constructed properly in the first place, or if the foundations were unstable then there was no hope of bodging together a decent, serviceable structure. In consequence it had been a very lonely summer. She'd still had the same need for warmth, companionship and love that she'd always had, but she'd started to feel that it might be easier and much less painful to be lonely than to be involved with some wreck who would without doubt come tumbling down around her ears.

Whether her father had been the pattern for her attraction to ruined men she couldn't be sure. Certainly he was in need of restoration work but that didn't necessarily mean he was a wreck. And certainly she'd had a child's desire to look after him, to be mother to the man, but she was no longer sure how much he'd needed her. She'd realized early on that as a father he was a mixed blessing, but from what she could tell at the time, and from what she'd learned about him subsequently, she didn't think he was actually self-destructive. Drink and drugs and madness weren't a problem for him, although women and children, she thought, occasionally had been.

She didn't really believe that his fascination with ruins was some metaphor for his own emotional or psychic wreckage. If anything she thought he might have found ruins a consolation. Yes, he wanted to create architecture but he must have known that, even if he'd succeeded, it would only have been a temporary manifestation of his talent. Sooner or later his buildings, like all others, however great or successful or admired, would begin to decay. They would be subject to the tyrannies of imperfect materials and changing taste and fashion. They might have been refitted or recycled, had new facades and extensions added, or they might simply have been abandoned. At last they would fall down or be bulldozed. If her father was a failure, she reasoned, then so was everyone else who had ever set one stone on top of another. Failure was inherent in the enterprise. She found this a consolation, though she wasn't sure her father ever had.

The sea at Monkwich was a dark, impenetrable medium, not because of its depth or dangers but because of sand that hung suspended in the water, turning it to a thick, brown broth, reducing visibility to inches. Somewhere in the depths were the crumbled, shuffled remains of a lost village. Since Roman times the sea had been biting off slices of the land, a yard or so each year, pulling the ground from under the houses, the inns, the farms, the churches. Divers went out from time to time, came back with lumps of church stone, sections of crosses smoothed by wave action, and they reported on all the World War Two debris down there still: shrapnel, unexploded bombs, the broken wings of bombers, all tangled in with the mess of domestic dwellings.

Kelly pulled the car into the broad, empty Monkwich car park. On summer afternoons this place would be jammed, but the kids had gone back to school, the holiday cottages were emptying and only a few stragglers and locals came to the beach. The snack kiosk was still open, but trade had slowed and it too would soon be closing for the winter.

They were there to see what remained of a medieval Franciscan monastery. Kelly had warned Dexter that the ruins weren't big enough or special enough to constitute a full day's entertainment, but Dexter wanted to see them, declaring a taste for both monasteries and ruins, so Kelly had taken him at his word.

The monastery ruins were a little way from the car park, in what was now a field at the cliff edge. Once it would have been a good mile from the sea. There was a perimeter wall that had originally marked out the monastery grounds but now it constituted the boundaries of the field, stone ramparts of unnecessary strength and substance.

There wasn't much left of the old monastery, barely enough to give a sense of how it had been. It consisted of little more than two parallel walls. The first wall was high and substantial and pierced by two tiers of Norman arches, and these had been heavily restored. While some small areas of the masonry looked truly ancient, with more mortar than stone in places, other sections had been recently rebuilt using modern bricks and modern building methods. The overall effect of the rebuilding was not so much unsympathetic as inauthentic, like a castle made of Lego. Parallel to this first wall was another, much lower, more solid, without arches or windows, obviously much later than medieval. It was built of old, irregular red bricks stacked together; orderly yet rough. Dexter thought it was worth a photograph. He muttered something about texture and colour, as though he needed to justify himself.

They circled the ruins, Dexter rather more slowly than Kelly. They both wanted to find the place inspiring and evocative, but the old stones refused to collude with this simple desire. They remained inert and inarticulate.

'As ruins go, it's a so-so ruin, I know,' said Kelly.

'I don't suppose they sell souvenir models of this,' he said.

'No, but there's a museum in the village, and they sell

95

little plaster churches, models of the ones that fell in the sea.'

Dexter was cheered, as though the day hadn't been entirely wasted. Kelly found herself irritated by this taste for souvenirs. Carrying away an artefact seemed more important to him than having the experience.

Dexter glanced up at the gloomy sky and seemed depressed. The day had started softly grey, but while Kelly and Dexter walked round the monastery ruins the sky had darkened and thickened, and was now threatening rain.

They walked through the field and on to a footpath from which they could reach the cliff edge. There was a thin tangle of saplings and bushes, a vain attempt to stop the land seeping away, and then there was the edge itself, a powdery, layered, red sandstone face that fell away sharply, fifty feet or more, down to a narrow band of beach below. Along the water's edge there were a few fishermen, each one alone with his thoughts and a heap of fishing tackle, and in some cases with an angular, black one-man tent.

Kelly read the signposts planted in the top of the cliff. They asserted the dangers of climbing up or down the face, warned about the fragility of the rock, but a small, stocky boy, about ten years old, in jogging pants and a black and white football shirt, was disobeying instructions and had climbed from the beach most of the way up the crumbling slope. Kelly looked down on him and churlishly thought he deserved all he got, though she suspected he wouldn't get what he deserved.

'I blame the parents,' she said archly.

And then it started to rain, one of those English showers that is hard, brief and drenching. There was nowhere to go for shelter and no point trying to run back to the car, since the rain would probably have stopped before they got anywhere near it and Dexter was naturally in no condition to run. It was one of those things that just had to be endured.

The small boy was now almost at the top of the cliff face and ready to scramble over the edge, but he was having difficulty and starting to look scared and miserable. The rain was soaking his shirt and the soft earth of the cliff face was turning to slush around him. He looked over his shoulder and glanced down at the beach a long way below. Suddenly he seemed to panic, to tremble, and he desperately needed to be back on firm ground. He twisted round, adopted a bizarre, stiff, upright posture, and tried to run down the sheer face as if he thought it was no steeper than a sand dune. He lost his footing almost immediately. His arms flurried and he just managed to fall backwards on to his bottom. The back of his head hit the cliff face and his hands reached behind him, scrabbling at the loose surface, which crumbled in his hands. His body became rigid and he started to slide slowly downwards, but as he descended a slab of the red earth cracked away and came with him. Rubble billowed around him like a wave, threatening to submerge and drown him in the miniature avalanche.

There was a slow-motion drift and fall as the boy descended perhaps two-thirds of the face. And then it was all over. He stopped sliding. He was firmly, ignominiously stuck, some ten feet up from the beach, his legs tangled in debris and sand. He was paralysed, too scared to move, and he began to howl.

Kelly and Dexter looked at each other and found themselves laughing out of embarrassment and relief. The boy was obviously going to be all right, and yet he was still in need of help. It seemed they should do something, though it was unclear what, given that they were at the top of the cliff and the boy was nearly at the bottom.

Almost immediately they saw one of the fishermen sweep into action. He ran along the beach shouting loudly and incomprehensibly, then made a brief, positive ascent to where the boy was stuck, and effortlessly yanked him out. His actions were fierce but loving, the actions of a father gripped simultaneously by anger, guilt and relief. He scooped the boy up and carried him away as though he were weightless.

Dexter and Kelly watched in silence. It was truly over now. There was nothing more to be done. 'Why isn't the little bugger at school?' Kelly wondered aloud. They peered down the cliff face at the place where the avalanche had started, the place from which the slab of earth had first fallen away, and Kelly saw something thin, white and brittle jutting out of the surface. Dexter saw it too, but was slower to make sense of the complex geometry of the thin bones revealed there.

'Is that really what I think it is?' he said.

'That depends on what you think it is.'

'It looks like a hand, a human hand. I mean a skeleton's hand.'

Silently Kelly confirmed that he was absolutely right.

'But how come?' Dexter asked. 'I don't understand.'

'We're standing on the edge of what used to be the monastery graveyard,' said Kelly. 'It stretched all the way from here to the sea. Then the elements took chunks out of the land, ate up all the graves too, washed them down with sea water. This hand belonged to some straggler who was buried at the innermost edge of the graveyard, in a grave that the sea didn't take away.'

'It's creepy,' said Dexter.

'It's just a hand,' Kelly replied.

'Shouldn't we do something about it?'

'Like what?' said Kelly. 'Pop down and collect it as a souvenir?'

'No. But shouldn't we tell somebody?'

'Who would you tell? The police? Do you think they have a standard procedure for dealing with this sort of thing?'

'So we do nothing?'

'We'll do something. We'll go and get a cup of coffee before the kiosk closes.'

Dexter shuddered grandly. Kelly found it surprising. She hadn't imagined he'd be so easily spooked. The rain had stopped by the time they got to the kiosk. They were served two cups of coffee that each came with a head of swirling, undissolved granules. They wiped off a couple of plastic chairs and sat down at a wet metal table. Dexter got out his hip flask and poured whisky into his coffee. 'You want some?' he asked. 'I'm not trying to spike your drink.' Kelly shook her head and watched as Dexter poured her share into his own cup. Then he said calmly and flatly, 'So tell me how your father died.'

The question was so plain, so apparently without tact or premeditation, that it disarmed her for a moment. She didn't know quite how to answer, yet she was perfectly prepared to. She looked at Dexter to see whether his question came out of interest and concern or just out of morbid curiosity. She persuaded herself that it might be the latter.

She said, 'There's an etching by Fuseli called *Artist Moved by the Grandeur of Ancient Rome*. It shows a figure, the artist, presumably male but actually strangely sexless, sitting down, holding his head in his hands. Behind him there are two giant fragments of the ruined statue of Constantine: one hand and one foot, each as big as the artist himself. There's something quite comical about the foot, like those *Monty Python* cartoons where a gigantic foot appears out of the clouds and squashes whatever's under it. But this particular foot of Constantine is earthbound – in fact, it's resting on a big plinth, but it still looks a bit silly. The hand doesn't look silly at all.

'They used that etching as the basis for the poster for an exhibition my father was involved with. The hand and the foot are as in Fuseli's original, but instead of a grieving male artist it has a great-looking, wild punkish girl staring at the ruins and laughing.

'My father loved ruins. He wrote about them a lot and he was invited to curate this exhibition. It was going to be held in a very hip London art gallery in Hackney, part of it indoors with photographs, plans, slide presentations and architectural models, and, outside, in the park, a handful of contemporary artists were commissioned to create modern, or I dare say post-modern, ruins.

'I've seen all the notes for the exhibition and I think it could have been amazing. There would have been stuff about Piranesi, about Babylon, about the Appian Way, about air raids. But there'd also have been sections on the architecture of derelict gardens, deconsecrated graveyards, haunted houses in the movies. And perhaps the outdoor section would have been best of all. There would have been a ruined city built out of children's building blocks, something based on the ruins of Pompeii, and the centrepiece was to be a re-creation of the exhibition poster.

'It could have been a great exhibition but it never quite happened. It was one of my father's unrealized projects, although I don't see that there was anything inherently unrealizable about this one. In this case it wasn't lack of money or vision or support that caused the project to be aborted. It was my father's death.'

She stopped and looked at Dexter again to see how interested he was. He was sipping his coffee and he didn't look as rapt as she wanted him to be, although by now it made no difference. She was unstoppable.

'The hand of death fell on my father,' Kelly said. 'Or, to be more precise, a concrete cast of the hand of Constantine as depicted in Fuseli's etching fell on him. It happened while the hand was being unloaded from the back of a lorry.

'My father had no need, no right, to be involved in the unloading but he was a very impatient man. It had been a real job getting the replica made, and on the day it was due to be delivered the lorry bringing it was hours late. The driver and his mate got lost coming through London. Then, when they eventually arrived at the gallery, they insisted on taking their tea break. My father had a big shouting match with the driver but apparently he got the worst of it since the guys went off and left him to it. But they didn't take the lorry with them.

'My father was furious and he ordered the wimpy assistants from the art gallery to help him unload this huge, incredibly heavy casting. They didn't know what they were doing any more than my father did. They messed about with ropes and pulleys but it didn't do much good. The concrete hand got caught on the tailgate of the lorry, and when, like an idiot, my father went underneath to try to free it, the assistants lost control of the ropes altogether and the hand slipped and fell and came crashing down on top of him. They say he was killed more or less instantly.'

'Oh shit,' said Dexter. 'I'm sorry.'

Kelly supposed it was as good a response as any, but she didn't react to it.

'Quite a bit was written about the incident,' she said. 'It made most of the papers. Everybody threatened to sue everybody else but in the end nobody did anything much.

The only practical action anyone took was to abandon the exhibition. It was said to have been done as a mark of respect, though I don't see what was so respectful about wasting all the hard work my father had put in. More likely there were people in the organization who didn't like my father, who wanted the exhibition to fail, and who were only too pleased to find a reason to abandon it.

'It was a stupid and unnecessary way to die, but I suppose the bizarre nature of it added to my father's mystique and dubious cult status. I guess all death's absurd when you get right down to it, and I think that dying with dignity is probably a contradiction in terms, but even so, being crushed by a concrete hand is a more absurd way to go than most. It's pretty hard to take seriously.'

She fell silent. Dexter was nodding gently as though some bothersome mystery had now been solved.

'Look at it this way,' said Dexter. 'It would have been even more absurd if your father had been crushed by the foot.'

'You think I haven't thought of that?'

She had, many times. She knew there were other much more silly, much more inconsequential ways to die, but how did that make any difference?

'I think my father believed that ruins have some sort of moral purpose, that they can teach us a lesson. But I think it's a lesson everybody already knows. The lesson is that nothing lasts: that you love somebody and they leave you; that you love somebody and they let you down; that you love somebody and they die. I think these things are worth knowing, although I think a person might know them without having to contemplate the ruins of antiquity.'

She felt she was about to cry. 'Oh, this is ridiculous,' she said. 'I'm too old for this. Come on, let's buy you a souvenir.'

In the museum there were fragments dredged up from the sea bed, pieces of gravestones and carved saints' heads, and in a glass case there was a scale model of the village as it had been before the sea ate it away. Dotted lines cut across the papier mâché land indicating the progress of the advancing sea edge. Dexter was pleased to find the plaster models of the churches that had fallen into the sea. He bought a St Nicholas, a simple, round-towered parish church, painted an improbable tan colour with a blue slate roof. He seemed well satisfied.

When they were outside he said, 'You're wrong, you know, when you said you should have got over your father's death by now. There's no should or shouldn't. And maybe you wouldn't even want to get over it.'

'Maybe.'

With great hesitation and some tenderness Dexter reached out a hand and patted Kelly on the shoulder. It was soft and asexual, and well intentioned, but Kelly pulled away instinctively.

'Is it time for that drink yet?' Dexter asked.

'Nearly,' said Kelly, 'but not quite.'

BUCKMINSTER FULLER'S BEDSPREAD

by

Christopher Howell

Just what is it that makes tomorrow's homes so different, so unappealing?

I remember the future. I remember how it used to look: so streamlined, so metallic, so (for want of a better word) futuristic. We imagined going to work by gyrocopter. We imagined being slickly conveyed by moving pavements and monorails. We imagined multi-level cities regulated by anthropomorphic robots.

Of course, some limited parts of this vision have come to pass. There are indeed a few very rich people who go to work by helicopter. There are moving pavements and monorails in airports, if nowhere else. And if we think of shopping malls as a new kind of city centre, then certainly they contain something preprogrammed and robotic, and I suppose traffic lights are robots by any other name.

But this is not quite what we had in mind. We imagined it would be more space age, and yet in using that term we acknowledge that the actual space age existed in a recognizable, limited, historical past.

Here was a future without patina. It had clean edges and hard, parabolic lines. There would be no time here for crafts, for earth tones, for things woven and shaggy. Hippies would have been a life form to be destroyed.

The future looked smooth, solid and cold, a place of metal surfaces and symmetry, a place where Daleks could run free. It looked like, and often was, a cheap science fiction movie. It was all featureless corridors, and metal doors that slammed down out of nowhere. The future was uncarpeted, unfluffy. It had no pictures on the walls. It glowed with its own inner light. Public and private spaces seemed identical if not undifferentiated. We imagined ourselves in lofty, voluminous spaces, dressed in stainless steel body suits. We imagined ourselves slim and severe and scientific.

The future was a place where we were in control, where tribes were united. Both the environment and human nature had been tamed, and therefore we could deal with some truly thorny problems, like invaders from other planets – not that they could ever prevail against our flawless technologies.

And yet in matters of popular taste, out there in the real world, there were those who thought the aliens were already amongst us, and that some of them were posing as architects. Some thought that Philip Johnson and Richard Neutra and Buckminster Fuller were not of this earth. And for many Americans, Buckminster Fuller was the scariest of all, since in so many ways he looked just like one of them, a Massachusetts' native, born in the last decade of the nineteenth century, a regular guy, tie-wearing, bespectacled.

In my lavatory, I keep a copy of the *House and Garden Book of Modern Homes and Conversions,* Editor Robert Harling, London, 1966. It's a largely photographic record of seventy or so 'contemporary' projects: a holiday home on the Sorrento peninsula, a converted London Transport sub-station, a Swedish waterside house shaped somewhat like a waterlily. And there amid all the glass and concrete, the teak furniture and the quaintly garish colour printing is Buckminster Fuller's 'Roam Home' in Carbondale, Illinois.

It's a geodesic dome, naturally, one of the ones made by the Pease Woodwork Company as a kit-home. It looks convincingly high-tech and industrial in an early sixties sort of way, and even though its appearance is less startling than some of Buckminster Fuller's more radical designs, it's still hard to imagine many people, then or now, actually wanting to live in it. Naturally, there's hardly a right angle in the place, nowhere that a sofa or wardrobe or bookcase would look genuinely at home, but one could argue that in the future sofas, wardrobes and bookcases might be redundant. Buckminster Fuller might well have argued that himself. But a look at the master bedroom of the house throws the whole conception out of kilter.

The bedroom is an oddly shaped, poky, irregular polyhedron, with lots of doors leading into the bathroom and walk-in cupboards, and walls sliced into strange angular slabs. And there, pressed up against the partition wall are two narrow twin beds in which Buckminster Fuller and his wife apparently slept.

And the beds have CANDLEWICK BEDSPREADS!

I ask you! Candlewick bedpreads just like I had in my own bedroom at home when I was a boy. Couldn't an imagination like Buckminster Fuller's have come up with something harder, shinier, more of tomorrow than that? Well, undoubtedly he could have, but the point is, he didn't.

In his own bedroom he demonstrated, even if he didn't admit it, that the human heart is not industrial and futuristic at all. It is not high-finish and aluminium clad; all that stuff is just something to fill the glossy magazines.

It's easy to see architecture and reality as metaphorically similar. Both, it might be claimed, are constructs. Both emerge from a collective, if multiform, unconscious. But that is surely the problem. The most startling architecture is constructed by those who are purist and visionary. Reality, however, is constructed by those who want something comforting, easy to live with and probably with a floral design. The future may not necessarily be candlewick (and pray God that it isn't) but neither is it likely to be elegant, clean-lined, restrained and concerned with the morality of materials.

We used to imagine that the future would include us. It would be us in the helicopter, us on the monorail. But as we get older, the one thing we know about the future is that it goes on without us. It is a favourite consolation of old age to imagine that the world has gone to the dogs, that it is in chaos and ruin and that things can only get worse. We tell ourselves that we are better off without the future, whereas the truth may well be that the future is better off without us.

7

Kelly saw herself in the mirror and thought she looked good. She knew she *could* look good given the right circumstances but she was never completely sure what the right circumstances were. Clean hair and enough sleep and the right amount of make-up had a lot to do with it but that wasn't the whole story. Bad hair days and sleepless nights didn't necessarily spoil the effect. Sometimes no make-up was good, sometimes a thick layer of slap got the job done. She felt she looked better now than she had done when she was younger. Her features had cleaned themselves up, become more defined. At twenty-five she'd looked better than at twenty, better at twenty than at sixteen. She'd never fetishized her own youth, though there had been others who had. But was she heading for some glorious late flowering, a perfect older woman, or had she already bloomed? Had there been a day, an hour when she could have gazed in the mirror and said, 'I look my very best at this very moment. This is as good as I'm ever going to look. It was all leading up to this one moment and it's all downhill from here.'? And if that was the case, when was that moment? How could it have passed unknown and unremarked?

When she arrived at the Phoenix Inn Dexter wasn't ready

to leave. He'd had a late night, drinking with the locals in the pub and now had a hangover. 'If you won't drink with me I have to find other people who will,' he said.

She took him to Orford, to the Ness, a long spit of grassland running parallel to the coast. They took a ferry across in the company of keen birdwatchers and a few restless, late-season tourists who didn't know quite what to expect. Dexter fell into this category.

'I guess we're not going across to see the wildlife, are we?' he said.

But he already had a shrewd idea of what was attracting Kelly. Visible on the Ness through the soft blue haze of distance was a group of bizarre structures. They might have been sinister garden pavilions, though they were too big, ugly and industrial for that. They had a concrete base, with a number of pillars along the open sides supporting a flattened pagoda-style roof. They seemed both purposeful and inscrutable.

'This land used to be closed off, some kind of military area,' Kelly explained. 'They told a lot of lies about what they got up to here. The story is they were just testing detonators. If the tests went wrong the pillars were supposed to collapse, blow out, and the concrete roof would drop down and keep a lid on the explosion. But I never really believed that.'

When they set foot on the land and walked round the structures, the story seemed even less probable. The wind whipped through the barren concrete pillars, long marsh grass swayed up to them like a tide.

'Are we talking chemical warfare?' Dexter asked.

'Who knows?' said Kelly. 'I always thought these would be great places to have sex. You've get the sea air but there'd be something over your head so you didn't feel too exposed.'

'You don't like to be exposed?'

'No.'

But there would be no sex here today, not while the birdwatchers patrolled the area with their binoculars and zoom lenses. And if you weren't a birdwatcher there was a limit to how long you could entertain yourself looking at enigmatic concrete. Kelly and Dexter were happy to return to the mainland.

'Is it time for that drink?' Dexter asked.

'Yes, I suppose it probably is.'

Kelly didn't like drinking in the middle of the day, hated that end of the afternoon feeling of not quite elation, not quite a hangover, but all the rules seemed to have changed over the last few days. She didn't intend to drink too much, but if she did, then what the hell, they could always call a taxi.

They went to a pub she knew: old fashioned, exposed beams, painted plaster, a real open fire, though they hadn't got around to lighting it yet. The place was almost empty, and it was cold. They were on their second drink when the door was hurled open and a drunken woman stumbled in. She was by herself and Kelly didn't recognize her at first, but she made straight for Dexter and Kelly realized she was the plump, flashy woman who had been part of Peter's group at the bungalow in Thorpeness. The woman apparently had fond memories of Dexter.

'Hello, Dexter,' she said grandly, then kissed him on the lips. 'That black eye's coming along nicely. Mind you, Pete's got one even worse.'

Dexter smiled. He thought he was quite a rogue. 'Hello, Jane,' he said. 'This is Jane. This is Kelly.'

They didn't feel the need to say hello to each other. Jane sat down opposite Kelly and tapped into a rich stream of drunken consciousness about men, sex and alcohol. It flowed fast and unmediated until the need for the last of these things reasserted itself.

'Let me buy you a drink,' Dexter said.

'Sure. Double rum and Coke.'

Dexter went to the bar leaving the two women alone.

'Sorry if I'm spoiling your little lunchtime rendezvous,' Jane said.

'You don't seem all that sorry.'

'Actually I'm not. This is a pub, right? A public house, not private, and I've as much right to be here as you have. More right probably.'

'If you say so.'

'Yes, I do say so. And I've a right to sit at this table if I want to and I've a right to—'

Kelly feared she might be about to enumerate a full list of what she considered to be her rights.

'Look, kid,' said Kelly, 'why not fuck off home and sober up? Or failing that why not just fuck off?'

If there'd been a drink in Jane's hand, it would no doubt have found its way into Kelly's face. As it was, Jane stood up empty-handed and looked as though she was about to burst into tears.

'You've no reason to think you're better than me,' Jane said blearily.

'Yes, I have,' said Kelly.

She got to her feet too and Jane stepped back, thinking she was about to be attacked, but Kelly walked away towards the bar where Dexter was still waiting to be served. 'Come on, Dexter, we're going.'

'Are we?'

He sounded confused, looked over at Jane who was now sitting lumpenly at their table, but that didn't tell him anything.

'Have we finished drinking?' he asked.

'I expect you'll have another drink at some point in your life.'

'Did you two have a fight?'

'Yeah, we both desired your body so badly, Dexter.'

Reluctantly Dexter followed Kelly out of the pub. He was limping badly now, and Kelly saw more clearly than she ever had before just what a conveniently variable condition it was.

'Come on,' she said, 'I've got something to show you.'

'Are we driving somewhere?' Dexter asked.

'No. It's near enough to walk, even for you.'

Kelly hurried along to the edge of the village, to a bridle path that went up behind the houses, between tall trees and rough hedges until it came to an ornate but rusted iron gateway. It was not locked and she pushed it open and stepped inside.

'What is this?' Dexter asked.

'It's a garden. Just a garden.'

They were standing on a track lined with unkempt bushes and undergrowth. It didn't look much like a garden. There were no borders, no lawns, no signs of care or cultivation. It seemed more like a patch of neglected woodland. It wasn't clear where the garden began or ended, and it was impossible to see the house to which it was attached.

'Whose garden?' Dexter asked, but Kelly only shrugged in reply.

She walked further along the track and Dexter followed, slowly becoming aware of odd things lurking in the untidy growth at either side of them. There were plaster heads staring up at them, broken columns made from painted wood. There were ivy-edged shards of broken mirror that caused uneasy glints and reflections, and peering from a swathe of ferns was a dragon made out of wire and plaster.

113

At the end of the path was a man-made archway, created by tying together the tops of two tall pine saplings. Vines and pieces of coloured cord had been strung from the curves of the arch and dangling from these tassels were shells, stones and old razor blades. They swung at a height that would hit a careless passer-by fully in the face, though Kelly ducked under them effortlessly and swept them aside for Dexter to pass.

They arrived in a circular clearing, about twenty feet across, various points of its radius marked by hefty white-painted rocks. These were irregularly shaped, and had been very carefully arranged, a job that would have required enormous effort and strength. Outside the circle, amid the trees, were taller piles of flattened stones placed one on top of another to form rough pinnacles and obelisks, and sitting on each pile, set in a messy little pool of cement was a different scrap object: a toy robot, a doll's head, a car headlamp, a model of the Eiffel Tower, a Coke bottle with a plastic rose in it.

'Is this art?' Dexter asked.

'Or is it just entertainment?' Kelly countered, and she was walking away again, out of the stone circle down another path. On the left was a fir tree, tall, shapely, neatly symmetrical. Things had been hung on it, as though it was a decorated Christmas tree, but the decorations consisted of wheel trims, pastry cutters, rusted spanners, bare umbrella frames, tin cans with top and bottom removed. There was some movement in the air and the metallic detritus swung and scraped together in a series of thin, unmusical sounds.

Kelly looked back at Dexter and saw him smiling uneasily, trying his best to enjoy this incomprehensible little adventure but not quite succeeding. His discomfort didn't displease her at all.

Up ahead something white was lying on the ground, something about the size and shape of a prone human figure; a very crude sculpture, not much more than a filled-in outline. But as they got closer they could see what had been used to make the sculpture – animal bones. There were thousands of them, some larger than others, but mostly very small; chicken and rabbit with a few sheep and cattle bones to create the main structure. They could also see that the figure was female. Two mounds of bones had been shaped into crude breasts, and between her legs where her pubic hair should have been was a clump of miniature roses.

Dexter reacted to a bad smell, something dead and decaying. He looked up into the branches of the trees above the bone figure and saw a dozen or more fox and squirrel carcasses hanging by their necks in little wire nooses. They were in various stages of decay, some very fresh, others reduced to a curl of ragged flesh on bare bones.

'Who designed this place?' Dexter asked. 'Mistah Kurtz?'

Kelly laughed. She had been coming here a long time. She knew the owner of the garden, an old man called William, a village eccentric, a weird, old, hard-drinking, somewhat feeble-minded recluse who'd inherited the house and garden from his mother years earlier, and for as long as she could remember he had been doing strange and wonderful things with it. He'd started simply enough making wishing wells and miniature versions of Stonehenge, but there was no doubt that he was getting weirder as he got older. Naked female figures and rotting carcasses were a new development.

They walked on, through more of William's handiwork: strange chairs made out of tree stumps and bed springs, privet bushes carved into jagged pieces of abstract topiary, a holly tree decked out with masks, strange bodies carved into

115

the trunks of trees, branches painted to look like snakes and penises, with nails driven into them.

At last they came to what Kelly considered to be the end, the focal point of the garden; a temple of sorts. It had started life as an ordinary shed or summerhouse but was much transformed. The outside had been coated with plaster, and while it was still wet fragments of tile, coloured glass and plastic had been set in it. Not quite content with this effect, endless little fetish objects had been attached to the walls and roof: old radio speakers, toy cars, lampshades, hats, spent fireworks – arranged randomly yet evenly all over the surfaces.

There was no door on the hut but lengths of barbed wire had been looped around the frame and it was not an inviting entrance. The pelvic bone of a cow was hanging above the doorway and arranged in front of it to form a perverse welcome mat was a neat expanse of broken glass.

'I'm not sure I like the look of this,' said Dexter.

'Oh come on, step inside the temple.'

She left him again and walked towards the doorway, striding swiftly over the broken glass and disappearing inside. Reluctantly Dexter followed. The inside was scarcely less strange than the outside though it was less cluttered. It had been thoroughly, meticulously lined with different types of fur, both real and fake. There were the pelts of rabbits and foxes, pieces of old fur coats, but also patches of lurid nylon car-seat covers in tiger- and pony-skin patterns.

'Is this supposed to be a womb?' said Dexter.

'Or a vagina,' Kelly replied.

Dexter took that as a signal. He moved close to Kelly and put his arms around her. She was surprised, though ready. She pressed herself against him and pushed her head back so her mouth was in place for him to kiss her. He was much stronger, more solid than she'd expected. She found herself flushing, her body feeling tense and liquid. She pulled her shirt out of her jeans so Dexter could reach up and touch her breasts, and after they'd kissed and fondled long enough her hand went down to his crotch, pressing and massaging, then she unzipped his fly and pulled out his penis. She was holding it fondly, working the skin back and forth when she heard an old man's voice behind her say, 'Hold it, hold it right there.'

The line was so unintentionally inappropriate that she couldn't help giggling, but she did immediately let go of Dexter's penis. Quickly but fumblingly he zipped up. Then, more slowly, they turned round and saw old William standing in the doorway. He was fiercely, dangerously drunk. In his hand was a shotgun, battered, rusty but quite possibly functional, and he raised it, eyeing Dexter and Kelly as though wondering which of them to use it on first. Although he was old, he was anything but frail. He had a heavy labourer's build, a broad chest and thick forearms. He was angry, and although his drunkenness was making him loose and imprecise, that didn't make him any less threatening.

'It's only me. It's Kelly, you remember me.'

It was apparent that he didn't, and even if he had it would probably have made no difference in his present condition. His kingdom had been invaded and he wanted to hand out punishment.

'What are you doing here?' he asked.

'We're just admiring your garden,' Kelly said.

'Is that what you call it?'

'It's a really nice garden, William. You've shown me around it before. You told me to come back any time.'

William seemed to remember nothing, and his anger wasn't abating.

'We weren't doing any harm,' Kelly said.

'You're bloody trespassers,' William said. 'And mucky buggers as well.'

'Not buggers,' Kelly corrected.

'I'm calling the police,' William said. 'They'll sort you out.'

'That's a good idea,' said Kelly. 'Why don't you go and call them. We'll stay here. We'll explain that we just wandered in by mistake.'

His face showed the workings of ponderous mental cogs and gears. Kelly's words hadn't had at all the effect she'd been hoping for.

'Yeah. You're right. Police'll be no bloody help. I should sort this out myself,' William said.

Kelly was still not really frightened. She assumed the cloud of anger would soon roll away and William would put down the shotgun and give her a good telling off as though she were a naughty schoolgirl. She might even have just pushed past him and run away, but Dexter's presence complicated everything. Finding two people in your garden was a lot more threatening than finding one, especially if they were having sex, and Dexter could not have run even if he'd wanted to, but she discovered that running was not Dexter's inclination at all.

William adjusted his grip on the shotgun, and Dexter chose that moment to act. He whipped his walking stick through a hard, flat arc and slammed the end with the crocodile against William's fingers. The precision was startling. The shotgun fell to the ground. Dexter moved forwards, swung the cane again, this time into the old man's face, causing him to yelp and grab his cheek. Then Dexter hit him in the belly, then across the side of the neck, then in the groin, and before Kelly could do or say anything, William was on the ground and Dexter was standing over him as though he seriously intended to crack the old man's skull open.

'Hold it, Dexter, hold it,' Kelly shrieked.

She grabbed his arm to prevent him using the cane to do any more damage. Dexter struggled. He was raging, and it seemed possible that he might turn on Kelly and attack her too.

'Jesus, Dexter. Please. Calm down. You'll kill him.'

Dexter let his walking stick drop, but his rage was still on him. He took a couple of deep breaths before he said, 'No old fuck with a shotgun is going to threaten me.'

Kelly stroked his arm as though trying to placate a dangerous hound.

'Or threaten *you*,' he added.

'For God's sake, Dexter, he's just a crazy old man.'

'An old fuck who slaughters squirrels and makes sculptures out of bones.'

Kelly wanted to think the best of Dexter. She wanted to put it down to cultural difference again. In America, if someone waved a shotgun at you he was probably a murderous psychopath. In England he was just a sad old man. But the savagery of Dexter's response still shocked her.

'It was another problem that needed fixing, so I fixed it, OK? Come on,' said Dexter. 'Let's get out of here.'

Kelly knelt over the old man to make sure he was all right. He was cowering, holding his arms round his head in anticipation of further punishment, but at least there was no blood, no evidence of permanent damage. She touched him gently.

'I'm sorry, William,' she said softly. 'I hope you don't remember too much of this when you sober up.'

She and Dexter left the 'temple' and hurried back the way they'd come.

119

'Let's go to your place and finish what we started,' Dexter said.

'You Americans amaze me,' said Kelly. 'You really do think sex and violence go together, don't you?'

He looked at her so blankly she knew there was no point trying to explain. They spent the night alone in their separate beds.

8

Kelly knew that it wasn't only Americans who made this connection between sex and violence. Like many women she'd been hit a couple of times by men she had reason to love, who had reason to love her, and being hit was undoubtedly a good reason to stop loving someone, but it was never that simple, even if you wanted it to be. But she never saw why people needed things to be simple. For her, complexity was always the attraction. She did not find herself suddenly attracted to Dexter because of what had happened the previous day with William, but the things that might have driven away a simpler, more absolutist, better, kind of woman didn't seem to apply.

It was the next morning and they were in Kelly's car again, and this time they were driving further north up the A12 to Great Yarmouth. Beethoven was on the stereo. A visit to a seaside town seemed both absurd and appropriate to Kelly. It wasn't that she was in need of the alleged benefits of sea air or seaside fun, but she had the urge to be a long way from certain aspects of the drama and violence of the previous day.

Dexter was apologetic, if not quite as remorseful as she thought appropriate. He had asked if there was anything he

121

should 'do' for old William, but Kelly had refused to engage in any such easy, secondhand solutions. If Dexter thought any action was required he'd have to come up with his own ideas. For her part she thought it best to say and do nothing, and to head for the coast.

In Great Yarmouth she parked on the promenade. It was a grey, flinty day, the air flecked with dampness. As the year cooled, Yarmouth was taking on that beguilingly neglected, abandoned air, although Kelly had known it to feel much the same in mid-summer. They got out of the car and Kelly started Dexter on what she thought would be a long walk for a man with a bad leg, all the way from the pier to the pleasure beach. There was a long row of boarding houses, and restaurants selling steak pie and chips. There were modern attractions, a sea world and a science fiction place where you were given electronic guns and chased each other round a fake warehouse in bad lighting conditions and tried to commit electronic murder. But Kelly had something much less technological in mind.

'Where exactly are we going?' Dexter asked.

'A little place I know. It's called "Small World".'

'What's that?'

'I suppose you'd call it a model village,' said Kelly. 'Right there.'

They were in front of a high fence and a locked wrought-iron gate that permitted glimpses of the miniature world they enclosed. Dexter paid and they went in. The place might have started out as nothing more than a fussy, over-elaborate garden. Curving paths forked and reforked, crossed and recrossed with a kind of manic energy, and between them were raised flower beds, rockeries, ornamental ponds. But the garden had been colonized by hundreds of miniature handmade models of men and women, none of them more than six inches tall. Around them had grown a frenzy of miniature buildings so that every island bed, every patch of lawn, had been developed and given small housing estates or hospitals, rows of shops, schools and recreational facilities.

It provided a detailed and not wholly inaccurate depiction of English semi-rural life, and yet it was a life lived at a pitch and with an intensity that was untrue to the real world. The village had more of everything than any real village would ever have: a fun fair, an airfield, a petrol station, a running track, a zoo. Everything was happening all at once; every activity was in full bloom. The football and cricket pitches were both in use. There was a bicycle race taking place on the outlying roads. There was a big wedding party gathering outside the church, while at the bank two masked robbers were making their get away pursued by the police. The milkman was making his round. The circus was in town.

But there were strange dislocations in this world. The bedding plants that sprouted beside the railway line were as tall as the signal box. The real goldfish in the ponds were bigger than the model fishermen trying to catch them. In the zoo, the size of the model animals was quaintly inconsistent. A pig might be the size of a lion while an elephant might be no bigger than a horse.

On the other hand, this was also a world plagued by massive real-life fauna. Birds as big as houses would descend and pull monstrous earth worms out of cottage gardens. Gigantic flies would settle on roofs. And when the rain came, a few big drops would be enough to soak the tiny immobile inhabitants.

Not absolutely everything was frozen. The sails of the windmill were turning, and a little electric train careered around a long circuit of track; but things were inert. The passengers at the railway station would never get on that

123

train. Those people crossing the road would never get to the other side. Those drinkers outside the mock-Tudor pub would never finish their drinks, never move from their tables.

Dexter looked around him with a kind of disdain. Kelly's latest expedition was a disappointment to him. This kind of fare was too humble even for a man with a bad leg and a professed interest in English eccentricity.

'Is this supposed to be therapy?' he asked. 'Yesterday was too exciting so today we do something as boring as possible.'

'Too much like family fun, eh, Dexter?'

'It's not what *my* family ever did for fun.'

'I didn't think you were ready for the white-water rafting just yet, what with your leg and all. Don't tell me you don't like it.'

'It's fine,' he said unconvincingly. 'I'll bet your father brought you here.'

'Yes. We used to come and play at being giants. We pretended we could shoot thunderbolts out of the ends of our fingers and we'd decide what and who to zap, and in what order; whether it should be the cricketers, or the old ladies on the bowling green or the drayman with the horse and cart.'

'I guess you had to be there.'

'Yes, maybe you did. It's all right for you, Dexter. For all your problems, you're going to finish up rich and comfortable, happily remarried to someone, working for the family business, or maybe some other business, but either way you're going to be just fine. Whereas I can see myself ending up somewhere like this, running some sad little seaside attraction, scowling at the tourists, shouting at the children who are enjoying themselves too much. But maybe you're right, a miniature village would be too tame. Perhaps I'd rather have something a bit more upbeat, like a crazy golf course.'

124

'Crazy golf?' said Dexter.

'Yes. That's the next part of your therapy.'

There were three crazy golf courses to choose from. One of them was newly built and had a pirates and treasure island theme, with concrete rocks and the fibreglass hulls of sunken ships, plastic palm trees and giant skulls and stretches of Astroturf for the greens. Kelly hated it. It wasn't only because it looked so synthetic, because, after all, how could a golf course be anything other than synthetic, but what she objected to was its store-bought blandness, its lack of soul and patina.

Half a mile or so along the promenade there was one she liked better, a much older course with an animal theme, each hole being presided over by a cheerful plaster animal: a smiling camel or a benign orang-utan. This place *did* have soul, in a faded, out of season sort of way; but Kelly had come to Yarmouth for the third course situated another mile or so along the promenade, on the very far edge of the tourist beat. There was something truly moving for her about this last place, a course that called itself Putting Land.

This was the one her father had always brought her to, and she still came back from time to time, always with the fear that it might have changed for the worse or even disappeared. But so far it had remained intact and constant, while getting increasingly scuffed and tatty, and it continued to thrill her. Putting Land consisted of just nine, cramped, interlocking holes, each involving some building or architectural feature. They were all made in a clumsily elaborate manner, and you didn't have to have a love of architecture to appreciate them, but if, like her and her father, you did have such a love then you were bound to be enthralled by the place.

Kelly was aware that she might be running Dexter ragged

by dragging him all the way along the seafront, but he didn't complain and she didn't care. A bit of penance would be good for him. In any case this trip was for her rather than him. But he managed to keep pace with her surprisingly easily. They stood by the entrance and Dexter reached for his camera.

'Come on, let's have a round,' said Kelly.

'I think I'd rather just take pictures.'

For Dexter a crazy golf course was something you might appreciate for its quaintness or picturesque qualities, and you might certainly photograph it, but it wasn't a thing you would engage with, much less have fun with.

'Oh, come on, Dexter, it's not as if you have to run around. You just have to stand still and hit the ball.'

'No, I don't think so.'

'Come on, Dexter, live a little.'

'Well, I don't—'

He still seemed a long way from convinced that this form of pleasure was for him, but Kelly wouldn't let him escape. She went to the kiosk, paid the old man inside – the latest in a long series of similar old men who'd held the job – and she returned to Dexter with two putters and two balls.

'Got a pencil?' she asked.

He reluctantly took the putter but was baffled by the request for a pencil.

'So we can keep score, Dexter,' Kelly explained.

'Do we have to keep score?' Dexter asked.

'Otherwise there's no point,' said Kelly.

Dexter looked sheepish. This was going much too far, entering too fully into the spirit of the thing, but Kelly found a pencil in the pocket of her leopardskin jacket and swept aside Dexter's hesitation.

They were the only players on the course, which pleased

Dexter since there was less room for embarrassment that way, not that there was anything remotely embarrassing about the first hole. The ball had only to be driven through the centre of a small wooden arch, painted to look like the Arc de Triomphe. If the shot was reasonably straight and accurate then the ball would go directly into the hole on the other side, although neither Dexter nor Kelly managed this simple job, taking a couple of shots each. Dexter handed his walking stick to Kelly before playing each shot and, despite his reluctance, she saw he was taking the game rather seriously. The way he stood, the way he held the club and addressed the ball suggested he knew how to play golf properly.

'Are you a golfer as well as everything else?' Kelly asked.

'Not really. My father made me have lessons when I was a kid, said it would be a valuable business skill. It was years ago, but I guess you never quite forget the basics.'

'Want to make the game more interesting?' Kelly asked.

'In what way?'

'If we had a little bet.'

'Money?'

'Not necessarily.'

'Then what?'

Kelly appeared to be trying to think of a suitable wager, although she already knew perfectly well what she was going to suggest.

'How about this for a deal?' she said. 'If you win the game you can have sex with me, if you lose you can't.'

Dexter laughed at the absurdity of the suggestion. 'What kind of bet is that?'

'Not such a bad one I'd say, Dexter. The fact is I can't decide whether I really want to sleep with you or not, can't decide whether it's a good idea or not. I suppose I could toss a coin, if you'd prefer.'

Dexter was amazed, as though he couldn't decide whether the offer was insulting or obscene.

'You'd really do that?' he asked. 'You'd let sex depend on something as stupid as miniature golf?'

Kelly didn't answer immediately and they walked on to the second tee.

'Sex always depends on something stupid,' Kelly said, 'like whether the guy's got nice eyes, or whether he's rich, or whether he pretends to be a good listener. Or it just depends on how much I've had to drink, or whether I can stand to go home alone. At least this way I'll respect you. I always respect a man who can handle himself on the crazy golf course.'

Dexter couldn't quite unravel the knots of mockery and sarcasm that lurked in that last remark, so he simply said, 'OK, it's a bet.'

The next three holes weren't so difficult: first a miniature log cabin with an open door at each end, then a lighthouse on the top of a low, gently sloping mound of plaster painted to look like rocks. Third was a dog kennel out of which poked an open-mouthed mongrel waiting to swallow the ball and pass it out through some unspecified hole in its rear, which protruded beyond the back of the kennel.

As he lined up the shot Dexter said, 'Do you ever wonder what it would be like if your father was still alive?'

'Of course I do,' said Kelly. 'I wonder how things would be for me, but I don't find that nearly as interesting as wondering how they'd be for him.

'I suppose it comes down to whether or not he'd ever have got to build any of his designs. If he hadn't, then I suppose he'd have become a very bitter man, but in certain circumstances I can imagine him finding the right people to work with. In one fantasy he finds rich, broad-minded

128

patrons all over the world. He builds wacky galleries and artists' residences in Southern California. In the Arab States he's employed to build desert palaces and pleasure domes, and in Japan he'd be constructing wonderful Zen-influenced hotels and apartment blocks, buildings made of plastic and rubber and carbon fibre. That wouldn't be so terrible.'

Dexter and Kelly took the same number of shots to complete the first four holes. Hole number five featured a free-standing railway tunnel, with one mouth going in and three exits on the far side coming out. The ball might emerge from any of these depending on the speed and direction it was hit. Kelly's familiarity with the hole was some help; she gained a shot by emerging through the right mouth to get directly on the hole.

'Then there's a slightly less highbrow, less intellectually respectable version of my father's future,' she said. 'I think it's possible he might have found a job in that area where architecture becomes entertainment. I think he might have worked in Las Vegas or Disneyland. Maybe he'd have done a casino in the shape of a space station, maybe he'd have designed a new city of tomorrow. Or maybe he'd have built white-knuckle rides. At the very least he might have designed crazy golf courses. That would just about have been acceptable.'

The sixth hole had a windmill. The ball was driven through an opening that pierced the base, but there were large revolving sails that intermittently blocked the way. Kelly's ball hit the sail and returned to the tee, and Dexter's score drew level.

At the seventh hole they were confronted by half a dozen miniature Egyptian pyramids. It looked easy enough to hit the ball between them but there were deceptive angles and areas of loose sand, bunkers of a sort, that made the hole fiendishly difficult. Dexter in his ignorance made light of these and pulled a shot ahead.

The pyramids were child's play, however, compared to the eighth hole which consisted of an open-sided suspension bridge spanning a shallow ditch filled with water. At first the task appeared to be to hit the ball straight and true so that it crossed the bridge and went on to the little circle of carpeted green on the other side. But the bridge opened and closed like Tower Bridge, and the shot had to compensate for the rising and descending inclines of the two halves of the bridge, and possibly the gap between them. If the ball went in the water it had to be fished out and returned to the tee. Dexter only made it across the bridge at the third attempt, but Kelly did far worse.

'Then again,' said Kelly, 'there's the nightmare version. My father might have ended up designing shopping malls, junk food restaurants, fancy cocktail bars and clothes stores. That would have been terrible. I'm enough of a snob to think that would have been a fate worse than death.'

'You've thought about this a lot,' said Dexter.

'I've thought about it far too much.'

As they came to the final hole Dexter was two shots ahead, not exactly an unassailable position, but a good enough lead to make him wonder how, when and where Kelly would offer herself sexually to him. The last hole, however, was so perverse and difficult that it could destroy anyone's lead, ruin anyone's good round. It was based on the Ruins of Pompeii and as Dexter set his ball on the tee he could see, some fifteen feet away, a three-foot-high replica of Mount Vesuvius. When the course had been in its prime, little puffs of smoke had emerged from the volcano's mouth, which was in fact the hole into which the ball had to go. However, between the tee and the miniature Vesuvius were a series of classical ruins of a maze-like complexity. A ball hit into their midst might ricochet off in any direction. Then, once the ruins had been crossed, the ball had to be driven up the ridged, steeply sloping side of the volcano and into its top. The volcano swallowed the balls and did not return them.

'Let me play through,' said Dexter. 'Let me finish my round before you start and then you'll know what you're up against.'

'Whatever you say,' Kelly agreed.

She found herself staring idly at the construction of the volcano. The chicken wire was showing through in places. The lower slopes needed repainting. Dexter made a pretty good fist of the hole, three shots to get through the ruins, one to get into the volcano.

'Not bad, Dexter, not bad at all,' said Kelly.

He allowed himself a little smile of pleasure.

Kelly took her ball, placed it on the tee, eyed the hole, effortlessly brought back the putter, swept it through a short arc and made brisk contact. Dexter couldn't tell whether the shot was deliberate or not, but the ball chipped into the air, appeared to spin and swerve, then began a swift, accurate descent right into the volcano's mouth. She had scored a hole in one. Neither she nor Dexter could quite believe their eyes, and they both said 'Shit' simultaneously.

She looked a little coyly at him, gave an apologetic flap of her hands. She'd won the round by a single shot. Dexter shook his head sadly and philosophically, as though this was precisely the sort of thing that happened to him the whole time.

'Look, Dexter,' she said. 'You really shouldn't be too disappointed.'

'I'm not,' he said unconvincingly.

'OK, you lost. So I don't have to sleep with you. But you

131

know something? The truth is I probably wouldn't have slept with you even if you'd won.'

'What?'

'I said we should have a bet to make the game more interesting. And it did. But I never said I'd honour the wager.'

Dexter was royally pissed off by this. He looked sad and wounded and depressed, far more so than losing a game of crazy golf, or even the prospect of sex, seemed to merit. Kelly took the putters and handed them in at the kiosk window.

'See you again,' the old man said.

They walked on to the promenade again, Dexter all brooding silence, until at last he said, 'Look, Kelly, I realize what I'm going to say will sound like absolute bullshit to you. I realize I haven't known you very long, and I realize you must get lots of guys coming on to you, but for what it's worth, I really like you.'

'Well, thank you, Dexter.'

She said it briskly and coldly, like a school teacher dismissing a child who has a crush on her.

'The fact is,' said Dexter, 'I think I could do a lot more than just like you. I'm pretty sure I could love you. In fact, I'm pretty sure I already do.'

'Oh shit, Dexter.'

She was embarrassed now. Suddenly Dexter seemed even more like a boy. He seemed naive and adolescent and very green. What he'd said sounded callow and groundless, and perhaps inappropriate, but it didn't sound like bullshit. Kelly knew that in some sense he probably meant it, and there was an old, not quite escapable magic in the words he'd used, even if she didn't think there was any way he could really mean them, or perhaps even know what they really meant. Having a man say he loved you wasn't an experience that came along every day, and it certainly wasn't something to be tossed aside without some consideration.

'We could discuss this over a drink,' Kelly said.

Dexter cheered up considerably. They settled in an empty, high-ceilinged, brown-walled pub and they discussed miniature golf and the English seaside. Then they talked briefly about Los Angeles and California and fear of earthquakes, until Kelly said, 'Sex is so weird, Dexter. When you're young it's so straightforward. You think you've got all the answers, and in a way you probably have. Then, as you get older, it gets so much more complicated, not that I mind complications in themselves—'

'What are you trying to say?' Dexter asked.

'I guess I'm trying to say, OK, you win. I've changed my mind. You lost at golf but you can still sleep with me. Is that OK? Is that a way we can both win? Let's go home to my place and get the job done.'

'Fine,' said Dexter.

There was too much traffic on the way back. Kelly drove with irritation and determination, getting stuck behind old ladies in their shopping cars. Delayed gratification did not have much appeal for her. She kept trying to imagine Dexter naked, wondered what his body was like, wondered whether he'd be inhibited about it, wondered if some change would come over him once he was in bed. She felt sure that Dexter would be horrified by her interior decor, but as he walked into the chapel he said, 'Cool place. It's just as I pictured it.'

'You must have more imagination than I give you credit for.' '

She poured them both outsize tumblers of Scotch, a necessary relaxant, and they began to make love. Dexter was far more passionate than she'd expected, and he was every bit as unhurried as she wanted. He kissed slowly and thoroughly and took his time. He filled the glasses again, and Kelly began to fear brewer's droop, but it didn't happen. They began fucking on the sofa of the living room, then moved gradually to the floor, then to the ladder leading up to the bed platform, then to the bed itself. Kelly noticed he brought the bottle of Scotch up with him. He took a mouthful and released it inside her vagina. A little fire burnt up through her. She wasn't sure she liked it, but she gave him full marks for inventiveness. The end was a long time coming, and the release was harsh and intense.

She said, 'That was pretty damn good, Dexter.'

He lowered himself beside her and said, 'Yeah, I was there.'

They both laughed and Kelly turned towards him and nuzzled her face into his chest.

'And another thing,' she said, 'when you're fucking, your bad knee doesn't seem to be a problem at all.'

She looked down at Dexter's legs, then sat up and began gently to massage them.

'So which is the bad one? The right?'

'Yes.'

She swivelled and moved her body to get a closer look, and found that both of Dexter's legs looked identically strong and healthy.

'They look fine,' she said.

Dexter didn't say anything, but he moved awkwardly in the bed, as though embarrassed, and he curled his arms round Kelly and drew her to him. Something was wrong.

'What is it?' Kelly asked.

'Oh shit,' he said. 'The truth is,' and he kissed her gently on the forehead as he spoke, 'the truth is, there's nothing really wrong with my leg.'

'What?'

'My leg's just fine.'

'What are we talking about here?' Kelly demanded. 'Sex as a miracle cure?'

She felt his arms tighten round her even more, and his whole body tensed up, as though he was frightened she might flap away.

'The truth is,' he said, 'there was never anything wrong with my leg. I made it up.'

Kelly laughed, a laugh that signalled both confusion and incomprehension. She really had no idea what he was talking about, but it crossed her mind that he might be confessing to some strange psychological condition.

'I made it up to get sympathy.'

'Did you really need to do that?'

Kelly tried not to sound accusatory but she was thinking how bizarre it was, an unnecessarily extreme way of provoking sympathy, and beyond that she wished Dexter might have waited a while longer before confessing it to her. It had rather spoiled the moment.

'I felt that I did,' said Dexter. 'For one thing it gave me an excuse to hire you for a whole week. If I'd been perfectly able-bodied you'd have thought it was pretty strange that I wanted to employ you like that.'

'I suppose I would,' Kelly said, trying to slow things down to a speed where she could understand the precise implications of what he was confessing to. 'But hold on, if your knee was all right then you had no need of a taxi anyway.'

The ridiculousness of the arrangement immediately dawned on her. Was he really telling her that he'd been faking the whole time, pretending to have a limp, pretending to have difficulties with stairs and shingle and getting in and out of the car? Why the hell would anyone do such a crazed thing? And she immediately asked herself what else he'd been faking.

'It was a way of getting close to you,' Dexter said.

'It was certainly that.'

Kelly extricated herself from his arms and drew away. She got up from the bed and put on her silk wrap. She felt alone and vulnerable and not at all sure who the strange man in her bed was.

'Let me get this straight,' she said. 'When I picked you up at the station that first night, you fancied me and so you invented the bad leg to give yourself an excuse for hiring me and spending time with me?'

She was trying to put the best possible gloss on things. It almost sounded attractive when she thought of it like that, a diffident man's fumblingly elaborate scheme to try to get the girl. Yet even as she entertained these charitable possibilities she knew that it wasn't going to be anything so simple or healthy.

'But that can't be right,' she said, 'because you already had the walking stick with you.'

'Yeah, I came up with the scheme long before I arrived in England.'

'You mean any taxi driver in any town would have done?'

'No. I only came here because I knew this was where you lived and that you drove a cab.'

'What?'

'I read all about you in a magazine. I saw your picture.'

'You're mad. Which magazine?'

'An interior design magazine. It showed you in this chapel. "Country doesn't mean conventional".'

Of course she remembered the article, but it seemed pretty unlikely that it had got all the way to the United States and that it had caused a man to get on a plane and fly to England

136

to pursue her. Besides, the article had appeared years ago.

'It wasn't that great an article,' she said.

'Well, I liked it,' he said. He shrugged and sat up in the bed. 'I have a bit more of a confession to make.'

'Haven't you confessed enough?' she demanded.

'My reasons for coming here were, initially, pretty suspect, I admit,' he said. 'Let's face it, in one way I'm just a parasite who's interested in you because I'm interested in your father. You see, I'm a great fan of his work – more than a fan. I wanted to meet you because I wanted to know more about Christopher Howell; and the subterfuge was necessary because I'd heard from other people that you'd stopped giving interviews about him.'

There was a dark, hollow silence before Kelly yelled, 'You shit. You absolute shit.'

'No, I'm not, really I'm not.'

'Yes, you fucking are,' she shouted. 'Get out of my bed. Get out of my fucking house.'

Her anger was incendiary and all-consuming. It was not to be argued with. Dexter got up from the bed, knowing he wouldn't be able to explain himself to Kelly at that moment, but feeling he had to try.

'But in all sorts of ways I'm not a parasite,' he insisted. 'And even if I was in the beginning things have changed. You've changed me.'

'Fucking get out,' she screamed.

She found some things beside the bed, thick paperback books, a hairbrush, a bottle of aspirins, and began to throw them at Dexter. He retreated to the edge of the platform.

'You don't know even half the story,' Dexter said desperately.

'I don't want to hear fucking stories.'

Reluctantly Dexter scrambled down the ladder from the

bed platform to the living room where he'd left his clothes. He began the awkward process of dressing.

'I have things to say that I think you'll want to hear,' he shouted up to her. 'Things that you need to hear. Please let me say my piece.'

He could hear her moving about above him and although he couldn't see her he carried on talking.

'You see, I'm a lot like you. I've always been interested in architecture. It's one of the subjects I've been studying, but obviously I couldn't tell you that because you'd have been suspicious.'

He saw that Kelly was now descending the ladder. He hoped she might be calmer, but as she came into full view he knew she was no less angry, and when she'd got down to floor level he saw her pick up what looked at first like a huge black serpent. It was the piece of driftwood they'd found on the beach at Sizewell. Kelly had managed to carry it into the house without anybody's help, and now she was wielding it as though she intended to impale him like a vampire.

Dexter spoke more rapidly. 'If I'd said I was an architecture student you'd have known right away I was after something.'

'Shut up, Dexter,' Kelly said, and she pushed the point of the driftwood snake into his belly.

'All right. All right. I get the message.'

'Good. Now get out.'

Still not quite dressed he scurried out of the house into the village high street. Kelly slammed the door satisfyingly after him. There was a three-mile walk to the Phoenix Inn but at least she knew he no longer needed to adopt a limp.

Kelly dropped the driftwood snake. As she locked and bolted the door she felt totally, depressingly sober. There were tears in her eyes and her hands were shaking as she sat on the floor and rolled herself a thick, strong joint. She filled her lungs with the smoke and stared up at the ceiling of the chapel.

She felt angry and used and stupid. She felt she should be better at all this stuff by now, a better judge of men, a better detector of lies and bullshit. Above all, she felt she should be better at not getting hurt, at not feeling this familiar pain. She was lonely, a sensation that was both specific and general, personal and universal. It was a loneliness that another person's presence could only dispel temporarily. Even if Dexter had not turned out to be precisely the sort of user he was, she knew he'd have still turned out to be a source of pain.

All the old chaos came flooding back. There was a need in her that she feared the mere presence of another person could never wholly satisfy. It wasn't about sex or love, it was about vacuity, hollowness. There was a big, empty cellar inside her, a void that could absorb and make irrelevant any amount of caring or affection that was poured into it. She recognized this and yet that didn't stop her needing, nor did it stop her trying to fill the void. It all seemed so familiar, so old hat. She knew, of course she knew, that this all revolved around the loss and absence of her father, and she knew it was time all that was over too.

She did what she often did at moments like this. She reached for her photograph album. It was in no sense a 'family' album since neither her mother nor her father had been interested in recording their lives, in documenting their pasts. So the task had fallen to her, pulling together snapshots from diverse sources, begging photographs from relatives or friends, occasionally writing to magazines that had published unfamiliar photographs of her father and asking for copies.

The album fell open at a shot of Christopher Howell

standing outside what looked like a log cabin, but was actually a motel unit. She assumed the photograph had been taken by one of his girlfriends. Kelly felt the intruding presence of the unknown photographer and it became a barrier between her and her father. She slapped the album shut. She needed something else, something more potent.

She got to her feet, determined but not highly co-ordinated, and she went upstairs on to the bed platform where there was a built-in storage cupboard she'd constructed. She opened it and pulled out a familiar cardboard box, removed some tissue paper and packing, and revealed the object of her fascination, her talisman, her last connection with her father, the one secret she had never revealed to any of the visiting parasites.

As a child she had called it her doll's house, though it was smaller than anybody's idea of what a true doll's house should be like, and no doll had ever lived in it. She hadn't been much of a girl for dolls. In reality it was an architectural model, a maquette, one that her father had made and given to her for her sixth birthday. At the time it had seemed a wonderful and special gift simply because it came from her father, but in retrospect she thought it was a strange present to give to a six-year-old girl, and at times she'd wondered if her father hadn't really made it specially for her, if perhaps he'd forgotten all about her birthday and had only come up with this as a desperate, spur of the moment thing, something he'd had lying around. Either way it made no difference. She had loved it beyond all reason and still did.

The model was small, on a baseboard that was no more than eighteen inches square, and it rose no more than a few inches from the board. It certainly couldn't be mistaken for anything other than a house, since it was surrounded by flowerbeds and a garden path, with a car in the driveway and a tiny postman delivering to the front door; yet it was hardly domestic. It resembled a mashing together of any number of different buildings, as though it was a collage of materials and features that had been found in some architectural junkyard and then brilliantly, if dementedly, combined.

There was not a single roof but a series of them: one a mansard, one in Spanish tile, one a steep lean-to, one flat, one a carved gingerbread-house arrangement. Also up on top of the building were various domes, minarets and chimneys that combined to create a roof-line as diverse and complex as that of a small city, scaled down to manageable proportions. Below the roof there was a piecemeal accumulation of doors and windows, more than seemed strictly necessary: bay windows, french windows, stained glass, some circular, some triangular, some simply blob shaped. There was stained glass in the doors too, and along one side of the house there were three doorways, each in a different style of English church architecture: one Norman, one Early English, one a Perpendicular four centre.

The walls were nowhere straight and they never met other walls at right angles. The rooms inside were wildly asymmetrical, often containing strange wedge shapes or oddly curved areas. The whole thing was embellished with curious features, some functional, some not: pillars, spiral staircases, balconies, flying buttresses, gargoyles.

The overall effect was of something ramshackle yet elegant, something primitive but of the future. The model represented a fascinating building with a fierce if unmalicious sense of humour. It was a beautifully, skilfully made model, detailed and delicate. It gave the sense of being made out of fragments and yet there was nothing fragile or sloppy about it.

If it had not functioned very well as a doll's house, it had still given great scope to Kelly's childhood imagination. She had fantasized about the life that went on inside it. This was no ordinary family house, she'd decided, at least not for the kind of family she knew. This was a home for heroes, for superheroes, for secret agents and film stars, and maybe for architects. And in her games she was all these things. She was Wonderwoman and Mata Hari and Emma Peel; and sometimes she was the architect too, the woman who had designed the building for her own special and particular needs, who lived there and occasionally, in a bountiful way, let in a few discerning members of the public.

But far more often her father was the true architect and she lived there with him, enjoying a life that was full and exciting and exotic, but still essentially warm and homely. Where her mother fitted into this, where she lived for instance, Kelly had never considered, but certainly not in the house.

Now she examined the model again, inspected it to see that nothing had become damaged or detached, and when she had reassured herself that all was well, that it was still hers and hers alone, she placed it carefully beside her bed, then lay down and curled up so she could stare at the model as she fell asleep, and thereby incorporate it in her dreams.

9

Kelly's sleep was dreamless, without travel to exotic cities or futures. She seemed only to have closed her eyes for a minute, but when she opened them again it was early morning. She didn't know the time, but it was just starting to get light; a soft glow of brightness seeped in through the window. The model of the house was as she had left it, though it looked somehow bleaker in the cold half-light.

She knew there was no chance of her sleeping again so she got up, pulled on some clothes and left her house. She got in the car, slammed one of her own tapes into the player and started to drive. The roads were empty and her head was still full of confusions and drink from the night before. Her concentration was patchy and she didn't know where she was driving to, but when she saw the sign for Monkwich it seemed as good a place as any other. The sky was big and distant, and the land fell flatly away from her on all sides. When she came to the coast she parked in the empty muddy car park, then went down to the beach. The tide was going out and the strip of sand at the water's edge was wet, so that her feet left shallow but distinct tracks as she walked along. Automatically she began looking for stones with holes through them, but soon gave up the idea.

Before long she sat down on the sand and saw, lying a few feet away, a child's bucket, the kind used to make sand castles. She picked it up, wondering whether it had belonged to a kid who was really upset to have lost it, or whether it had been thrown away in some fit of wastefulness and indifference at the end of the holidays.

She found herself kneeling on the beach and absent-mindedly filling the bucket with sand. It was clammy and solid, and it got under her nails, but it felt good. And when she tipped the bucket out she found she'd made an almost perfect little tower: solid, smooth, nicely proportioned. She repeated the process several times, and before long she had built a little circle of towers, the beginning of a city. She dug in the sand with her hands, creating canals and rivers between the towers and she moulded a ring of city walls around them, and then she moulded little igloos, and an amphitheatre and a couple of pyramids.

She moved on to the decoration, pressing stones and bits of shell and feather into the sand walls. By the time she'd finished her task the sky was a light, cold, optimistic blue and a pale sun had bobbed up beyond the horizon. She stood up, brushed the sand from her hands, then from her knees. She surveyed what she'd done, and concluded that it looked a complete mess. It had no style or design or flair. It was dismal and pathetic. A child would have done better.

Slowly and with a carefully honed appetite for destruction she brought the heel of her boot down into the centre of the nearest sand castle. She watched it start to split and crumble, and then she put her full weight on it until it was completely flattened. More swiftly she did the same to the next tower and the next, until none was left standing, then she dragged her instep across the boundary walls and the other structures so that they collapsed and filled in the canals and rivers.

A voice behind her said, 'Having fun?'

She didn't have to turn round to know it was Dexter. Just the sound of his voice was enough to bring on feelings of anger and nausea.

'Look what the tide washed in,' she said.

'It wasn't the tide brought me here,' he said.

'Then what the hell did?'

'I got up early. I borrowed a bike from the landlord at the Phoenix. I went to your house. When you weren't there I had to think of where you might be. I figured you wouldn't be at Sizewell, and I didn't think you'd have gone to Thorpe-ness. I thought you might be here. I was just guessing. But I guessed right.'

'You're such an intuitive bloke, aren't you, Dexter?'

She turned her back on him and walked away from the ruined sand city, heading further along the beach. The sun was now glinting off the dome of the nuclear power station visible just a few miles up the coast.

'Please give me a chance,' Dexter said miserably. 'I've been up most of the night. I couldn't sleep.'

He tried to put his hand on Kelly's shoulder. It was done hesitantly and it wasn't threatening, but Kelly revolved like a weathervane and as she spun she lashed out with her clenched fist and landed a punch right between Dexter's eyes. His mouth dropped open in pain and surprise, and he toppled over backwards, landing oafishly on the sand.

Kelly was at least as surprised as Dexter and she had to fight the urge to kneel beside him and ask if he was all right. But she did notice that he'd dropped something he was carrying – a black leather portfolio that had fallen away from him and was in danger of being soaked by an incoming wave. Without thinking, she retrieved the case and held it out to him, but Dexter wouldn't take it.

'Now that I have your attention,' he said groggily, 'I want you to listen for just one minute. Just one minute.'

Kelly didn't want to listen, but it was true, he did have her attention, and it was surprisingly hard to walk away from a man you'd just knocked to the ground.

'First,' he said, 'whatever you think about my original motives for coming here, they changed the moment I met you.'

He paused to catch his breath, but Kelly was aware there was something rhetorical about it too. It was a device to make sure the next thing he was about to say stood alone and was given its full importance.

'It's true, I *am* a fan of your father's work,' Dexter said. 'And that doesn't make me a monster. I've been interested a long time, longer than I ever realized. And I think I've made an important discovery. You know the famous article that referred to your father as the greatest modern English architect who never built a building.'

'Of course I do,' Kelly said.

'Well, he was wrong. Your father did build something.'

Kelly stared at him. Had he really said that?

'Open the portfolio,' Dexter said.

She looked down at the leather case in her hands and realized she was trembling. She fumbled with the zip until she'd got it undone all the way, and then she stopped, hesitated, unsure that she wanted to open it up and see what was inside. She had no idea what it might contain, but whatever it was she thought it was likely to be scary and threatening. Perhaps her father had built something terrible – a torture chamber, a slaughter house – or something truly banal and trivial – a gazebo or a petrol station. But she spurred herself on. She had to see what had to be seen.

The portfolio contained a sheaf of clear plastic display pages and inside each one was a glossy eight by ten photograph. They were black and white images, very crisp and sharp, very professionally done, and they showed a building in various states of completion. First there were the foundations being dug, then poured, then a frame being erected, then walls and sections of roof being put in place. Only very slowly did the building take shape in the pictures; and at the same pace Kelly realized what she was seeing.

The house being built in the photographs was a full size version of her childhood doll's house, her birthday present, her talisman, her final, undisclosed secret. The last few pictures showed the finished article, the completed building, the model that had become actuality.

The photographs were cleverly taken and dramatic. Low viewpoints and wide-angle lenses made the house look grander and more startling than she suspected it really was. But there was no doubt that this was a part of her past, her imagination made solid. She realized it must also be an even larger part of her father's past and imagination.

She sat down on the sand beside Dexter. The world was swirling, and the sound of the sea had suddenly become deafening.

'Did my father really design and build this? You're certain?'

She had to be sure there wasn't some mistake, that it wasn't perhaps a house by another architect that her father had simply reproduced to make her doll's house.

'I'm sure,' Dexter said. 'I have documentation.'

'Why didn't you tell me sooner?'

'I don't know. I guess I was waiting for the right moment.'

'After you'd fucked me?'

'That was never part of the plan.'

147

'So what was the plan exactly?'

'To get close to you, to win your confidence, get you to talk about your father, then spring this surprise on you and see how you'd react.'

'Was this supposed to be some sort of psychological experiment?'

Dexter looked ashamed. 'Maybe I thought I could get an article out of it, get something published in one of the less academic architectural journals. Maybe I thought it was a way of making my own reputation.'

'You're such a piece of scum, Dexter, you know that?'

'I'm not so bad. Really.'

She looked at the photographs again, lingering over some interior shots. These were spaces that she had previously only imagined, but it seemed she had imagined them quite accurately. The rooms were consciously stark and bare, very interior decor mag, very unlived in; finished but not humanized. Builders were visible in the early photographs: sixties characters with bare chests, long hair and headbands. And yes, it seemed to be in some foreign unfamiliar place, obviously not England. The light was harsh and bright, there were faded mountains in the distance.

'You must be quite a researcher,' Kelly said. 'How the hell did you ever manage to track this place down? Where is it?'

'I've known it most of my life,' Dexter said. 'I've lived in it. It belongs to my family. It's the vacation place I talked about, in the desert, in California.'

'Oh shit,' said Kelly.

'My father always liked to think of himself as some sort of patron of the arts,' Dexter explained. 'He had too much money. He liked to commission young up-and-coming artists and designers, though he wasn't much older himself. Some-how or other he met your father at just at the right moment.

148

I guess he must have been fresh out of architecture school, and my father employed him and told him to build whatever he wanted. We called it the "Cardboard House", I was never absolutely sure why. I think it was some sort of reference to an essay by Frank Lloyd Wright, something about organic architecture.'

'This is too much,' Kelly said. 'This changes everything.'

'I don't think my father liked the finished house very much. There was some sort of dispute about money or materials or earthquake regulations. He said the building was ugly and too hot, that sort of thing, but when I was a kid I didn't care about all that stuff. To me it was like a fun house.'

'You liked living there?'

'I loved it.'

'But why didn't my father acknowledge it? Why did he keep up the pretence that he'd never built anything?'

'I don't know,' Dexter said. 'I was sort of hoping you could help me with that.'

Kelly didn't speak. She couldn't. Tears were running down her face, dripping from her cheeks on to the clear plastic display pages. She tried to wipe them away with sand-stained fingers. Dexter watched her and wanted to help. He wanted to put his arm round her but he was now far too wary to risk an attempt at consoling her.

He said, 'I thought you'd be pleased.'

'You have no idea, Dexter,' said Kelly. 'You really have no idea.'

'What do you want to do now?'

'I think I want to show you my doll's house.'

'Huh?'

II

THE NEW

'Any house is a far too complicated, clumsy, fussy mechanical counterfeit of the human body. Electric wiring for nervous system, plumbing for bowels, heating system and fireplaces for arteries and heart, and windows for eyes, nose and lungs . . .'

Frank Lloyd Wright, *The Cardboard House*

MOTEL AMERICA

by

Christopher Howell

Those who remember the plot details of *Psycho*, and surprisingly few do, may recall that it begins not in the Bates Motel (which is, in fact, an improbably homely establishment despite its taxidermy collection), but in a far sleazier place where Janet Leigh is having a lunchtime tryst with her married lover. She complains about having to meet in these low-rent surroundings, and this more than anything propels her towards stealing the bag of money from the real estate office where she works, which in turn propels her towards the Bates Motel, Anthony Perkins and her fate.

In fact there is a strange stylistic discontinuity in the film between the Victorian Gothic of 'Mother's House' and the more standard, insubstantial architecture of the motel itself, but together they reinforce the idea of architecture as threat, the haunted house plus the motel room, two mythic spaces where terrible things happen to people.

When *Psycho* was made in 1960 the Holiday Inn chain had been in existence for a decade or so and was doing well, but it still had only a few hundred franchises, and it would be two years before Motel 6 came into existence, offering a similarly standardized but much cheaper product. Most travellers in 1960 who needed a bed for the night had to take their chances.

As far back as the 1940s, in a more or less deranged article that J. Edgar Hoover wrote for a magazine called the *American Nation*, he claimed that motels were places where criminals hung out, where illicit sex was freely available and where it was easy to buy drugs. The simple response to this is 'only if you're lucky'. But in motels you do have a tendency to get lucky.

I, needless to say, think it has something to do with the moral dimensions of architecture. The best motel architecture looks not merely playful but actually trivial, as though to say this place is unreal, what you get up to here in this fun house doesn't really count, it's outside your real life. You won't be held responsible for what happens here. And so you're free to have illicit sex, to take drugs, to consume beer and potato crisps in bed, to watch mind-numbing television. You are free to behave like a sleaze.

You wouldn't behave like this if you were staying in some high-class Venetian palazzo, not even if you were spending the night in a good old-fashioned seedy English bed and breakfast, but to engage in bad behaviour in an American motel is to partake of the truly American experience.

Transience and anonymity, these are the great American virtues. Tomorrow you'll have moved on and put it all behind you. Everyone remembers the horror of the Bates Motel but there are many worse motels in America, and I'm sure that if Janet Leigh had been able to check out the morning after she wouldn't have found it so terrible at all.

My favourite is the Rocket Motel in a place called Frontier Town in the Mojave desert, geographically not that far away from Palm Springs, but a million miles away philosophically. Frontier Town itself was built in the 1940s as a sort of permanent movie set. A property speculator reckoned there'd always be somebody who needed a place to shoot a cowboy movie so he built Frontier Town, a place with greater solidity and authenticity than sets usually had, and for a while he did good business. Then cowboy movies became less popular and the town declined until the 1960s when hippies decided Frontier Town had just the kind of surreal trippiness they were looking for. A group of them moved in, refurbished the place, and they or their successors are still there now.

The Rocket Motel consists of half a dozen gloriously inauthentic, free-standing log cabins, and above the check-in office is a sign consisting of a neon rocket ship trailing a burst of stars. The cute proportions of the cabins, the brilliantly eye-catching incongruity of the sign, the fact that it's in the desert in a town that was built as a movie set, suggest that this is a place where nothing authentic, nothing consequential, could ever happen. One can behave badly here with complete impunity and on my few visits I've done my very best to live up to this architectural imperative.

The Rocket is my favourite, but it isn't my ideal. For that I envisage a thousand-unit motel, built somewhere mythical and metaphorical, like Timbuktu or Alice Springs or Xanadu, and each of the thousand units would be built in a different architectural style. First there'd be all the usual motel imagery, the tee-pee, the railway carriage, the motel court, but then there would be cabins in the shape of mud huts, miniature Palladian villas, geodesic domes, pagodas, cricket pavilions, bathing huts, beach huts, grass huts, gazebos, igloos, bedouin tents, lighthouses, gingerbread houses, tea houses, tree houses, bottle houses, boat houses, gate houses, Ashanti fetish houses, aeroplane hangars, mosques, parish churches, castles, crofts, windmills, miners' shacks, Tudor cottages, Swiss chalets, Bauhaus cubes, fall-out shelters. There would be units showing the influence of Vanburgh and Boulée, Mies van der Rohe and Christopher Wren, Louis Sullivan and Louis Kahn, Vignola and Palladio, John Nash and Edward Zander. And in each and every one of these units every guest, whether singly or in pairs or in groups would be acting very, very badly indeed. It would be a kind of Arcadia.

10

Kelly made a phone call to her mother.

'I'm going away for a little while,' she said.

'Another holiday?'

Kelly hadn't been thinking of it as a holiday, but she said, 'Sort of.'

'It seems to me your life is one long holiday, Kelly. Going somewhere nice?'

'The States.'

'Oh *really*?'

Her mother now found this holiday a topic of passionate interest since she knew that romance and intrigue, a man, had to be in there somewhere.

'Is Dexter taking you?'

'I'm taking myself.'

'But you'll be there with Dexter?'

Kelly wanted to deny it. It sounded so obvious, so mundane when her mother described it and yet what was the point in lying; that only granted her mother even more power.

'Yes,' she conceded. 'I'll be there and Dexter will be there. But it's not quite like that.'

'Like what?'

'It's not some cheap holiday romance, like I met a rich American who swept me off my feet and now he's taking me home with him.'

'Then what *is* it?'

What indeed? How could she explain, to her mother of all people, that she felt compelled to go with a strange man to a strange place in a strange country, in order to look at a building that her father had built? Why couldn't she say what was really on her mind? 'Look Mother, I'm travelling six thousand miles on the off chance of feeling some sort of connection with my dead father. I know it sounds crazy, but that's the way I am.' Yet how could she change the habit of a lifetime?

She might also, although only if she and her mother had been two completely different people, have asked her if she knew anything about this strange house in the Californian desert built for the Dexter family, the Cardboard House, as she now knew it to be called. Yet it seemed obvious that her mother didn't know anything. If she'd known then surely she'd have mentioned it at some point over the years. As family secrets went it seemed quite devoid of shame or embarrassment, yet it appeared to be a secret her father had kept totally to himself. Then again, another, a better, daughter would no doubt have wanted to share this discovery and revelation with her mother, whereas Kelly wanted to hug the information to herself, to wrap herself in a private intimacy with her father.

'You're right, Mother, it's a holiday romance.'

Her own reasons for subterfuge were simple enough to understand, but her father's seemed far less explicable. She could come up with possible reasons but she couldn't tell which ones applied. She could see there was a neatness, a philosophical purity in being the greatest modern English

160

architect never to build a building. It had more clout, more cool, than being an architect who only ever built *one* building. But another, more uncomfortable, possibility was that perhaps this building in California just wasn't very good. It looked fine in the photographs and as a maquette, but maybe it didn't work in reality. Perhaps it had been a failure and her father had simply wanted to forget about it.

Kelly said to her mother, 'You know when you said that Dexter reminded you of Dad, what was it about him?'

Kelly's mother tried to sound dismissive. 'Oh, I don't know, something in his manner, perhaps something in his eyes. Nothing very serious.'

'I realize this is a silly question but did you think Dexter looked like he might be a bit . . . dangerous?'

'All men are a bit dangerous if they're remotely attractive. That's why women are attracted. Not that women can't be dangerous too.'

It sounded like a confession.

'You thought my father was dangerous?' Kelly asked.

'Dangerous but not fatal. Not to me, anyway.'

'And George?'

'No, George wasn't dangerous.'

It felt as though they were straying into an area of emotional revelation. Silence fell like a dropped blanket.

'So you and Dexter are an item?' her mother asked breezily.

'I've slept with him if that's what you mean, but as a matter of fact I don't plan on sleeping with him again.'

'So you're flying to America to be with a man you're not even going out with?'

'It's not like that.'

'It's all right, Kelly, I understand.'

'No, you don't.'

'All right then, I don't.'

161

'Good. I'm glad you realize that.'

'But I don't know why you're so pleased not to be understood.'

11

Kelly was embarrassed to be so excited by the prospect, even just the idea, of travelling to America. All her self-possession melted away in the face of the mundane business of practical arrangements. Packing, getting the train to London with Dexter, checking in at the airport, killing time, going to the duty-free shop, the hectic lassitude inside the plane, all made her feel eager and vulnerable. She was glad though, and a little surprised, that Dexter didn't condescend to her.

He had described the shape of the journey: a long plane ride in a jumbo jet to Los Angeles, picking up a hire car, then a night in an airport hotel, then the next morning a three-hour drive out of LA into the Mojave where the Card-board House stood in its own patch of desert. It sounded clear enough and not really very complicated, yet parts of it felt so vague, so faint. What would the hotel room look like? Would it be scary to be out in the desert? How hot? Would there be sandstorms and rattle snakes? Would she feel sick or scared or overjoyed? The house itself she couldn't even think about.

She enjoyed the sense of reversal. The guide had become the guided. She had, with some success she thought, shown Dexter her bit of England, even if all along she was being drawn towards some location, some final landmark that was of his choosing, not hers. Now he was taking her to his territory but for a purpose that was hers, and in which he could only participate tangentially.

She was glad she had no responsibility for the trip. She was anxious and distracted enough, and perhaps that was fortunate since it also distracted her from judging Dexter, from examining the implications of his behaviour, his lies and the use he had made of her. She was tolerating him because he could take her to her father's house. The question of whether he was, in more normal circumstances, tolerable was for now beside the point. Later she would weigh him and, she felt sure, find him wanting, but her inevitable condemnation did not yet need to be converted into action. Wait till your father gets home.

It was hard for her to get used to a Dexter who didn't limp, who didn't use a walking stick. Even though she hadn't always been sympathetic to his condition, it had always been a presence, it had defined her perception of him. She found herself sitting in the thin plush of the airline seat, wondering if there was enough room for his bad leg.

Dexter was not a relaxed or easy flying companion. He was fidgety and restless. He demanded a lot from the air stewardess: extra booze, extra napkins, extra pillows. She was pleased when he fell asleep.

The free drink kicked in and she felt confident and capable, strong enough to deal with the troubles, and who knew, maybe even the pleasures, that lay ahead. It would be strange and difficult, but not impossible. She sensed she was at the beginning of something, and its end was a million years in the future. And what would happen once she'd seen the Cardboard House? She had no idea, but it didn't seem to be too important. Departure didn't matter, only arrival. She

164

hoped she would be a different person once she got to the house, changed by an as yet inconceivable experience. Setting foot inside her father's building felt like the end of the reel. What came after that was improvisation and invention.

She watched the movie, looked at the clouds, thumbed through the in-flight magazine and then she slept. She only woke as the crew were serving the afternoon snack, the indication that landing wasn't far off.

'Now, about where we're staying,' said Dexter. 'Do you have any serious preferences?'

'You told me you'd booked somewhere already.'

'I have, but bookings are made to be altered.'

'I really don't care too much,' said Kelly, 'so long as there aren't stains on the sheets and so long as we have separate rooms.'

'We'll have separate rooms for sure if we go where I'm thinking.'

'What are you thinking?'

She felt angry. Why did he want to start changing things? It was so typical. She should never have trusted him. Inevitably he would be difficult. Inevitably he'd want there to be complications.

'We could stay with my father,' he said.

'Oh,' said Kelly.

She felt unbalanced. She couldn't imagine Dexter at home with his father. She knew there was a family business, and it wasn't as if she wanted Dexter all to herself, but she was used to seeing him operate in isolation and she didn't welcome change.

'I thought you might want to meet my father,' said Dexter. 'I thought you might want to meet the man who commissioned your father. I'm sure he'd be able to tell you things about the Cardboard House.'

'We'd stay in his home?'

'Right.'

'I don't know.'

'It's an interesting house.'

Everything seemed suddenly to be doubt and indeterminacy. Yes, of course she ought to want to meet her father's patron, there would undoubtedly be things to learn, new information to be gleaned, but at the same time it would be another obstacle, another screen between herself and her desires, another delay. She felt the pressure of too much data. This wasn't some school project. She wasn't concerned with showing she'd done the right amount of homework.

'Well, anyway, I called him before we left London and he's meeting us at the airport,' Dexter said. 'At least we should go have a drink with him. You wouldn't mind doing that, would you? He's a pretty cool guy.'

'I mind you springing this on me at the last minute.'

'Yeah, well, you probably mind a lot of things about me.'

'And I really don't think I want to stay in your father's house.'

'OK, so tell him when you see him.'

But how could she? She knew she wasn't brave enough to be that rude. She felt newly, doubly resentful of Dexter, and disappointed in herself for being so feeble.

'It's all right,' said Dexter, though he didn't sound reassuring. 'He's just a father. I thought you approved of fathers.'

She supposed she did, though she supposed also that her approval was neither here nor there. She didn't know what to expect from Dexter's father. She knew from what Dexter had told her that he had to be rich, but what did that sort of alien, American wealth mean? How rich was rich? Would there be a chauffeur, a limo? And what would he look like? Would there be a face lift, a nose job, a tummy tuck?

166

In fact, when she saw him at the airport in Los Angeles, on the edge of the small crowd of meeters and greeters, he looked a lot like Dexter, but there was something odd about the look. She'd been prepared for him to be an older version of his son, yet in some curious way he looked younger. While Dexter put effort into looking solid and substantial, his father worked at looking light and youthful. He was tanned and slim and he wore faded, expensive jeans and a pristine white shirt. His hair was grey but it was abundant and artfully styled, and although his face was creased with age, the creases seemed to be evidence of how much he smiled rather than of how careworn he was. He was making no obvious attempt to look like a man of stature or substance, and yet you could tell that was precisely what he was.

He didn't walk towards them but stayed firmly planted where he stood, letting the world come to him, and when Dexter and Kelly got close he said, 'Hello Jack,' in a soft, friendly voice, and it took Kelly a moment to realize he was talking to Dexter, who seemed as unfamiliar with this use of his first name as she was, and she saw him wince. Before her eyes Dexter became more callow, less sure of himself.

'Hello, Dad. This is Kelly.'

'Hi, Kelly. I'm Bob.'

Dexter's father smiled. He had charm. If she had been in the market for a house she felt sure she'd be prepared to trust this man. 'Hello,' she said in return, and she wanted to sound substantial too, grown up, to show she was here for something serious, but she heard her voice come out sounding too thin and girlish for the occasion.

'You *are* going to be staying with me, aren't you?' Bob Dexter said, and although it was a welcoming, easy remark, there was an imperative there too.

He took Kelly's hand and folded it gently in his, a handshake of sorts, then picked up her bag, a pink and black holdall bought specially for the occasion, which now seemed very cheap and tacky to her. She considered hanging on to the bag, insisting she could manage perfectly well by herself, and if she had ever been going to say that she'd be spending the night in the hotel this was obviously the moment. But she found herself not saying it, not saying anything at all.

Then they were outside the airport building, walking through thick Californian afternoon sunshine. The world looked sharp and clearly outlined, deep blue and green. There were palm trees, for God's sake! The brightness hurt her eyes and the angle of the sun looked all wrong. Where was the pollution and yellow smog? She felt weak and vulnerable as she got into Bob Dexter's car but the thick leather seat fitted round her, making her feel not comfortable exactly, but at least supported. And then they were heading away from the airport, through light but fast-moving traffic, and she was glad to have said nothing, to have made a choice only by default. She stared at the reassuringly serious dashboard of the car, at the sky outside, at the sharp skyline of glass towers, and again she felt glad to be far away from home and freed of responsibility.

Dexter and his father made only the thinnest, most perfunctory remarks to each other and she rather liked that. If they could be uncommunicative so could she. If they demanded nothing from each other then they could demand nothing from her.

The world outside the car looked strange but no stranger than she'd been anticipating. She watched the traffic. She felt the reassurance of the power steering, the power brakes, the soft changes in the automatic transmission. The roads were wide and straight, and if the drivers didn't appear utterly relaxed, at least they kept up an appearance of being cool.

Flashy, improbable cars drifted past: Corvettes, Mustangs, restored and lacquered classics, moving money, the sort of wealth that was clean and fun.

Then they were driving up into hills, and the car was taking tight, fast bends, and the land was rising steeply on either side of them. There were big houses but they were set back from the road, clandestine, only partly visible, screened by hedges and walls.

She wondered what kind of house Dexter's father lived in. She had been prepared for something utterly preposterous and palatial. A man who, when young, had been rich enough and reckless enough to commission a house on his own patch of desert might have ended up living in any kind of giddy monstrosity, but somehow she already knew it wouldn't be monstrous at all. Bob Dexter seemed to be nothing if not tasteful.

He stopped the car in front of a solid metal gate, which slid back in response to a remote control and they went in to park on a short chunk of driveway. The house stood before them and Kelly thought it was wonderful. It was a single-storey post-and-beam pavilion, a wide, low, horizontal building that sat lightly on the earth. It was flat roofed, and full-length glass walls rode in a frame of steel squares. The sun was streaking the glass pale orange.

'The place was built in the early sixties by a student of Richard Neutra,' Bob Dexter explained. 'Not one of his very best students, but still . . .'

They went inside. It was smooth and bare, cool open spaces with redwood walls and floors, and built-in leather couches. There were some gaudy yet severe abstract paintings on the walls and a couple of African masks, but nothing that looked remotely personal.

Kelly found herself saying, 'Do you live here all alone?'

'Afraid so. But I'm always open to offers.'

She found herself smiling politely, pretending to be amused, and then she felt that perhaps she should be insulted, that this was a crassly sexual remark, a wholly inappropriate bit of flirtation. Like father, like son.

The more she looked around, the more obvious it became that Bob Dexter did indeed live alone, and had probably lived that way for a long time. There was a chilly, masculine emptiness about the house's elegance, something bleak. She felt a sadness for him, a sadness that grew as she was shown into the guest suite in a distant arm of the house.

The room was impersonally clean and ordered, with a shower that had individual portions of soap and shampoo just like a hotel. It was a guest room that received all too few guests. She was given time to clean herself up, and it felt like a commandment to wash away the grime of travel, and perhaps of her past life. She obeyed. She stood in the shower for as long as she could, delaying the moment when she would have to go out and meet up again with Dexter and his father. There had been talk of going to a sushi bar or of sending out for gourmet pizzas. It all sounded too difficult. She wondered how long she could stay in the shower, in this private world of water and glass, how long before it would be considered rude, how long before they'd tap on the door to ask if she was all right in there, how long before they'd break down the door to see if she'd collapsed.

She emerged at last, in creased clothes, her hair still wet, her face pink, and she could hear Dexter and his father not far away making stilted, polite conversation. She followed the sound of their voices to the kitchen. The place astonished her, so bright, so spotless, widescreen windows, brushed aluminium, as though no one had ever done anything as messy as cooking there. Father and son were sitting at a black

170

marble counter and they were drinking wine. Three glasses and a wine cooler were set out in front of them, and as she hesitated in the doorway Dexter's father filled the third glass and said, 'This one's got your name on it, Kelly.'

Kelly took the glass. She felt she was being offered a magic potion, the elixir that gave access to a new world, where fathers were rich and lived in some style and shared alcohol with their troubled adult sons.

'Now you can open the present,' said Dexter.

At first Kelly imagined he was speaking to her and she saw the small, wrapped package on the counter by Dexter's elbow, but it was not for her. Dexter's father took the package and cautiously unwrapped it, peeling through cardboard and tissue paper till he reached the contents. He looked and smiled. He had unwrapped two miniature buildings, the beach hut from Southwold, and the church of St Nicholas from Monkwich.

'There was another one,' Dexter said, 'of a strange little folly called the House in the Clouds. I don't really know what happened to it.'

Kelly didn't choose to tell him.

'These are great,' said Dexter's father. 'Really great.'

Dexter began explaining their provenance, describing his travels with Kelly, regurgitating some of the information she'd given him, information that had mostly originated with her father.

'And if I'd had my way,' Dexter said, 'there'd have been a model of a nuclear power station too.'

'This is plenty,' his father said, and he smiled ever more broadly. 'This is fine.'

He was more pleased and amused by these small gifts than Kelly thought he had any right to be. They were nice enough holiday souvenirs but not so very special surely, and she guessed they must have a private meaning she was not party to, a family joke. She felt excluded, and unsure whether or not that was intentional.

'Some buildings are called follies,' said Dexter's father, 'but if you want my opinion they're *all* follies. Owning property, whether it's a town house or a condo or a tar-paper shack, is just insane. And even if you're not insane when you start out you're sure to be insane by the end. Property just drives you crazy.'

Kelly remained silent. Property ownership was a subject she knew nothing about, and she preferred it that way.

'And as for building a house from scratch,' he continued, 'that's a very special, malevolent form of madness, and anybody who seriously thinks about doing it ought to be locked up.'

Was it the flight, the jet-lag, making feel her so delicate, so easily offended? Or was she justified, and were Dexter and his father playing some nasty little game with her? Had she been brought here to be ritually, if casually, humiliated? Surely Bob Dexter was insulting her father, his work and his memory.

'I'm not really blaming your dad,' he continued, reading her. 'He was very young, very inexperienced and I really wasn't all that much older, and I sure as hell wasn't any wiser. I had too much money, and even though we were trying to be hippies, there wasn't much peace and love. We were two arrogant young sons of bitches and neither of us was the visionary genius we both thought we were. Neither of us got what we wanted, but maybe we both got what we deserved. It was definitely a learning experience, whatever the hell that means.'

She tried to pick her way through the scrub of self-deprecation, insult and hindsight to tease her own meaning out of what he was saying, but she couldn't think quickly or clearly enough, and then he was unpacking more information.

'What did I think I was doing? I look back and I really have no idea. I guess maybe I was trying to be a Renaissance princeling. And I was trying to impress some woman; my then wife, Jack's mother. I wanted her to think I was a hell of a guy. At the very least I wanted her to think I was in control of my own destiny. Well, we all know how that worked out.'

Kelly *didn't* know, of course, but his manner, his little snort of exasperation and fatigue said a great deal.

'I guess if I'd been the great rich man I thought I was I'd have employed John Lautner or Buckie Fuller or somebody, but they were kind of occupied. So I used your father instead. He also had the great advantage of promising to be cheaper, though I don't think that necessarily means anything much, and in the end he wasn't cheap at all. And together we *learned*.

'I learned that having a house built for yourself is a great way to lose money and not get what you want. And I guess your father learned that he wasn't cut out to be an architect. In retrospect, I figure those are things well worth knowing.'

To Kelly it all sounded too glib and finished. She wanted to come to her own conclusions, and it sounded as though he wanted her to share his.

'I'll show you something else I learned too,' he said.

He finished his drink and got up from the counter. He beckoned for her to follow him and, while Dexter stayed in the kitchen having another drink, he led her through the hall to a door that went into the rear of the house. They

173

entered a small, bright office, infinitely less stark and ordered and much less 'designed' than the rest of the house. There was a lozenge-shaped table at the centre of the room, stacked with untidy piles of books and papers, and the walls were lined with cluttered, stuffed bookcases. There was some impressive-looking computer hardware, business machines, a big screen television.

'Look around,' said Dexter's father, so she did, at the rows of art, photography and architectural books, glossy coffee-table volumes mostly, though they'd been well read and there were endless slips of paper and dog ears marking pages in them. And then she saw a big glass vitrine, museum style, that lived by the window, displaying a collection. Inside were scores of miniature buildings: tiny versions in metal and stone, plaster and plastic, glass and crystal, of all manner of famous buildings. There was the Colosseum, the Taj Mahal, the Chrysler building, the Coit Tower. There was a group consisting of multiple versions of the Empire State Building and the Statue of Liberty. There were collections of Sphinxes and Eiffel Towers and Seattle Space Needles, miniaturized versions of St Peter's Basilica, the Brandenburg Gate, the Hoover Dam, the Lion Fortress. There, in easy reach, were the Kremlin, Antwerp Cathedral, the ruins of Hiroshima City Hall. There were buildings as paperweights, as inkwells, as salt and pepper shakers, as cigarette lighters, as bookends; buildings as clocks and thermometers. There were ashtrays in the shape of stadiums, banks in the shape of banks. There were generic, idealized log cabins, thatched cottages, Greek temples, diners, pyramids and pagodas. And each one of them could be easily held in the palm of one hand.

Kelly looked and she found herself laughing. There was something so frivolous about taking such huge edifices and reducing them to ornaments. She thought that Bob Dexter must be quite a joker to have assembled this metropolis of souvenirs.

'The thing I learned,' he said, 'is that wanting to control the world is a pretty soul-destroying task. The world has a way of getting up and biting you in the butt. Asking your father to build a house for me was an act of youthful hubris. I thought that if I had my own little patch of land and my own little house I'd be in control of everything and that would make me happy. The fact was I couldn't even control your father and the contractors and suppliers. It was too hard. I was no good at it. So that's why I started amassing these things.'

He opened the door to the vitrine, picked up the Sacré Cœur in one hand, and a section of the Great Wall of China in the other, and weighed them against each other.

'These things I can just about manage to keep under control,' he said.

She thought of the model of the Cardboard House, still on the bed platform in her chapel back home, and wondered if perhaps it belonged here with all its stunted cousins.

'Your father and I fell out in the worst way,' said Bob Dexter. 'We fought about everything: the design, the materials, the way he worked, the people he employed. We argued about art and we argued about money. It was a mess, a nightmare. But, let's face it, that was a long time ago. And we weren't exactly the first architect and client ever to have a disagreement. We got over it. I came to have fond memories of him. I was pretty devastated when I heard he'd died like that.'

What could Kelly say? That she was sorry he'd been devastated?

'I sincerely hope you're not going to be disappointed when you get there,' he said gently. 'It's a long time since anybody

175

lived in the Cardboard House. I couldn't even guarantee it's all still standing.'

He must have seen the pained expression on her face as he said that, but he continued, as though wanting to prepare her for the worst.

'And frankly, the house wasn't exactly perfect when it was brand new. So you could be disappointed.'

She felt defensive, of herself, of her father, of his building, but she didn't feel weak. She said, 'I think I'm expecting to be disappointed. In fact, in a way, I think I want to be disappointed.'

Dexter's father nodded. 'You're smart,' he said.

He put the Sacré Cœur and the Great Wall of China back in the vitrine, and closed the glass doors.

'You know, some of this computer technology is pretty scary,' he said, slapping his hand on a monitor. 'They can do computer modelling of just about anything. You could take some of your father's unbuildable buildings, put them in the computer and go for three-dimensional tours around them.'

'I'll settle for the real one just now.'

'Yes, you're smart.'

Dinner was eaten at an austerely fashionable restaurant close by. Kelly felt uninvolved in what was happening around her, as though watching a cartoon. It was all two-dimensional and brightly coloured and inconsequential. She felt tired out yet manic, fascinated but unable to concentrate. She found herself ordering food she knew she didn't like.

Dexter and his father talked about people she didn't know, about things she didn't understand. There was some discussion of the real estate business – Bob Dexter had recently sold a house to a hot young movie star – and there were several mentions of Dexter's ex-wife. It appeared Bob Dexter was still in touch with her, had eaten lunch with her. This seemed to count for something, to demand some response from Dexter that he was unwilling or unable to give.

After the food, as they drank decaff, Dexter's father placed a key on the pristine white cloth of the restaurant table.

'For you, Kelly,' he said. 'It opens the door to the Cardboard House, the door in the Norman arch.'

She took the key. It felt cold and looked too big for any domestic door. She gripped it tightly until it had taken on the warmth of her hand. She wanted to cry. She was barely aware of the drive home, and then she was back in Bob Dexter's house, in bed, and it seemed to be the next day.

The dust storm moved in, a swirl of sand that enveloped her and then cleared, and a mountain became visible: steep, inhospitable, rising like a crusted brown molar from the desert around it. They were driving. Dexter was at the wheel of some decrepit military vehicle, wearing goggles, his face and hair matted with dust, Kelly strapped in beside him.

They came to the base of the mountain, to a flight of steps cut into the rock, a frayed rope for a handrail, and suddenly Dexter was gone and she was alone climbing up and up the steps, the treads getting narrower, the rope getting flimsier, birds of prey circling overhead. Her legs were like soft rubber. There were bleached bones on the mountain side, the teeth of dead critters, but it was all right, she was in the right place, being drawn to her father's house which was up on this mountain top. She felt she'd been there before, the route gouged in her memory like a line drawn in the dirt, up these last few steps, over the rim of the summit, and she knew she'd soon be there. She would see the house. It would reveal itself, throw open its doors and winch her in.

And there it was, she saw it, her father's house, the Cardboard House, exactly as she'd imagined, exactly like the model she knew so well, and then she was looking down on it as though from an aeroplane. The space in front of her rippled with heat, played tricks with distance and perspective. The house seemed so small from this height, so far away, it looked like a toy. The light was flat, sunless, soft and shadowless, yet for all the tricks of distance and heat, the house was truly revealed. And that's when she realized it *was* only a toy.

She had come all this way to discover that the little doll's house her father had given her was an absolutely exact replica of the house itself, in one to one scale. Here on this mountain top he had built his only building, but as another architectural model, a maquette, as something a child could pick up or stamp on or toss down the mountain side or turn into a home for birds or desert lizards.

She felt betrayed (though by whom?), homesick, woozy, barren, and she turned around hoping for support, for something enveloping and upholstered like leather car seats, and all she saw was Dexter and his father, and they were laughing at her. This was their punchline, the whole point of the experiment, to see how she'd react. They were slapping each other on the back in what seemed to her a crude, fake display of manly father and son bonding; and only then did she notice they were both naked, well, naked except for ornate black cowboy boots, and they both had springy, absolutely identical erect penises.

Everything became softer then, and curiously consoling. She understood. Only a movie; only a dream; only the backwash of anxiety, the scrambling of charged possibilities; and as she turned over in the strange bed, turned her back on the mirage, she knew this had been an act of potent, strengthening magic. She had imagined the worst, the most trivial.

She knew that when she got to the desert, the house would be there, not absolutely as she imagined it, not absolutely as it appeared in the glossy architectural photographs, but it would be real and important, not just a fantasy, not a bad dream brought on by jet-lag and unfamiliar food. Her time would not have been wasted, and Dexter and his father would not be standing behind her offering up their identical erections.

She felt as though she hadn't slept, but suddenly she was awake and it was late and she could smell coffee and hear male voices. Now everything seemed rushed and difficult; getting washed, getting dressed, the hurried, ham-fisted repacking of her bag. She wanted to be up and out of there, on the way to their final destination. Drinking coffee and eating a perfunctory breakfast and saying goodbye to Bob Dexter, only a temporary goodbye he insisted, all took much too long for her tastes, and even though she knew it was only a few hours' drive to the Cardboard House, the delay seemed to threaten the whole enterprise. What if the car broke down on the way? What if they had a crash? What if Dexter lost his way?

At last they were travelling in a shiny red pick-up truck borrowed from Dexter's father. She hadn't imagined him to be the kind of man to own a pick-up but it was just another thing she didn't understand, or need to, and in truth it was a clean, pampered vehicle. The interior of the cab seemed needlessly plush, the stereo unnecessarily high quality. Dexter chose to play Haydn.

The sun was still hurting her eyes. The surface of the freeways was blindingly white. She put on sunglasses so that the world retreated a couple of shades. It didn't feel as though they were leaving Los Angeles but rather as if the city itself was retreating, gradually slipping away from them, reducing in density, becoming sometimes suburban, sometimes industrial, until eventually the buildings would thin out completely and the desert begin to show through.

She looked at it all, at the curvature of bridges and exit ramps, the busy disorder of gas stations and fast food restaurants, apartment houses and motels, and it was simultaneously familiar and disorienting. Yes, she had known it would be more or less like this, she had seen enough movies, and yet from England it had all seemed mythic, or at least fictional. To see all the clutter of roadside architecture made real was to see it lose some of its power.

She looked at the car washes and strip malls, buildings stranded in expanses of car park, edged by roads without pavements. There was an empty lot with a glorious sign that said, 'Will Build To Suit'. She imagined being alone on foot somewhere in this low, flat, inhospitable complication and she felt lost and isolated.

'Your father seems like a very nice guy,' Kelly said to Dexter.

'Yeah, he does seem that way, doesn't he?'

'Meaning?'

'Meaning that people seem different to their sons than they do to the rest of the world.'

'But you were in the family business. You wanted us to stay with him. You must like him.'

'Must I?'

After a couple of hours' driving, they stopped for petrol on a blank stretch of road, and even the petrol station was disorienting, offering strange cultural challenges, strange-looking pumps, payment required in advance. They appeared to be absolutely nowhere, just a desert roadside, but the desert wasn't quite as she'd anticipated. She'd imagined it only as absences and vacancy and yet the territory around her was not empty at all. There were abandoned shacks, now without roofs or doors or windows and yet still four-square and sturdy, and in the distance, set back a long way, were ranch houses, one of them with a geodesic dome. There was a lot of clutter out there in the emptiness.

Finally, or at least penultimately, they were no longer on the freeway, not on any sort of main route, but heading along a dwindling empty road that curled between low, scrubby mountains. The lower slopes were scattered with single buildings, surprisingly elegant bungalows with pitched, red-tiled roofs and double garages, and then the land flattened, opened up and there was a sign that said, 'Welcome to Frontier Town'.

Up ahead, set back a few hundred yards from the road, were two rows of buildings, a cowboy main street, the former movie set with some houses, a saloon, a church, a jailhouse, all built of wood, with an unpaved road running between them ready for the shoot out, and there too was the Rocket Motel, the one her father had described in his article, six quaint little log cabins and an elaborate neon sign on the office with its trail of stars.

Dexter parked in the dirt beside the saloon. It called itself the Rocket too, though its name was painted on wood, not etched in neon. Dexter sensed Kelly's bafflement.

'Believe me, Kelly, this place seems as strange to me as it must to you.'

Kelly couldn't come up with any words, but she nodded, finding his disorientation reassuring.

'We're really pretty close now,' he said. 'The house is about ten miles or so up the road. I could do with a beer before we get there.'

Kelly didn't know what she wanted. Delayed gratification

had been no part of the plan, and yet an interruption, a pause in the syntax of the journey, now seemed appropriate and welcome. They headed for the Rocket Saloon.

The interior was darkly cavernous, filled with the chilly flap of air conditioning; a clustering of tall, wide rooms, their exact dimensions and shapes deceptive. Apparently it had once been a kind of themed cowboy bar with saddles and pictures of Roy Rogers. They were still there, but recently there had been other influences. It was now bedecked with techno-hippie paraphernalia, wall hangings in imitation of the work of threatened tribes, an oil painting of Jerry Garcia, photographs of desert sunsets and fractals, a small stage at the end of the bar and a wall of fame with signed, framed photographs of unknown rock and country performers. In the far corner was a kitchen and a sign that said they served food at any time of day or night: steak, chicken, Texas burgers, pinto beans. Kelly and Dexter were the only customers. A tough-looking young woman served them with bottles of beer, and Kelly slumped on her stool, elbows on the bar, sullenly peeling the label off her beer bottle.

'How does it feel?' Dexter asked.

'I don't know. How *should* it feel?'

'You're free to feel any way you like.'

She said, 'I wish I was already there at the house, but I'm scared of being there. I wish it was over but I don't want it ever to be over. Sometimes I think it would have been better if you'd never even told me about the house. But I don't really think that.'

'This is a weird place,' Dexter said, looking round the saloon.

'Yes,' said Kelly. 'I like it.'

'It used to be a real dive but every few years it changes hands and the new owners do some remodelling and build on an extra couple of rooms. I guess that's what people do.'

He became aware that he was talking to himself, that Kelly had drifted away into her own, more elaborate, world.

'I was thinking that maybe we should check into the motel now,' he said.

Kelly looked confused as though this was an impossible suggestion, as though the Rocket Motel was a place of fable, a site you might visit, but not a place you would actually stay.

'Why?' she said.

'Look, Kelly, I know this is a big deal for you but the truth is, the world isn't going to end the moment we get to the Cardboard House. We're going to have to spend the night somewhere or other. I suppose we could drive back to LA, but something tells me you might want to stay around for a while, take more than one look at what your father made. Go back tomorrow. See it again. Hang out.'

Kelly said, 'I suppose you're right.'

'And your father did write kind of interestingly about the Rocket Motel.'

They finished their beers and went to check into the motel. Business was slack and they had their choice of log cabins. The woman in the office found it touching that they wanted separate rooms. Even if she hadn't read 'Motel America' she knew this was not a place people usually came to be chaste.

If the outside of the cabins tried to be rustic and cute, the insides tried to be garishly, datedly exotic: a blue vinyl headboard, carpet the colour of German mustard, plastic tongue and groove on the walls, a peacock etched into the mirror, a print of a coyote above the bed. Kelly dropped her bag on the shiny, quilted counterpane and was ready to go out immediately. Acclimatization was neither necessary nor possible. She would never feel at home here, nor would anyone else.

Then they were in the truck again and Kelly strapped the seat belt across herself, as though she was finally settling into a rollercoaster. The white-knuckle ride was in full motion. She had to grit her teeth and hold on.

It was a long ten miles, through land that became increasingly threadbare. Frontier Town was the last late burst of civilization before the Cardboard House. She carefully watched the truck's milometer creep round, saw the tenths of miles slowly adding up, and she didn't understand why they couldn't see the house yet, and then she *could* see it, not the whole house at first, just a familiarly complex roof line, a hint of shape and outline that could only be the Cardboard House.

Dexter put his foot down and the truck's tyres bit into the earth, bouncing over rocks and sand, and soon the house was wholly visible. It was raised up a little, held on a low pedestal of grey and red rock, so that she saw it from below, a view she'd seldom had of her doll's house. It was so familiar yet so strange; just the sight of the doors and windows, the way the walls fitted together, the way the balconies and gargoyles hung off the edges of the building. When they were still about a hundred yards away Dexter stopped the truck, turned off the engine, said, 'I think you should go the rest of the way by yourself.'

'Why?' said Kelly. 'Don't you want to see my first reaction? Wouldn't that be good for your article?'

Dexter said nothing.

She unfurled herself from the cab, landed awkwardly on the sand and began to walk towards the house. She felt like a pilgrim, a tourist, maybe like a prospective house buyer. She had been quite prepared for the house to be incomplete or badly damaged, for chunks of it to be broken away or falling down. Perhaps, she thought, it would have been appropriate to discover it was a vandalized ruin, although she sensed that would have been too neat and easy. Most surprisingly of all possibilities it looked whole and intact, and just as she'd imagined it.

Then she felt as though she was approaching an information desk or a visitors' centre, the first room of a museum where she might find a useful introduction to the subject, a place where there'd be maps and leaflets, a short video programme, postcards for sale; her father's life commemorated and explained, made simple and digestible. She thought of her mother alone in Suffolk and felt a soft, unworthy sympathy for her.

The house looked neglected but not abandoned, and not so much decayed as gently faded. There were no flowerbeds, no paved driveway, no cheery postman, as in the model, but that was all right. For all the intensity, for all the strange luggage of confusing emotion she was dragging with her, she found herself smiling. The house made her happy. The match between reality and maquette was perfect, and for a second, as though in a different dream, she was no longer sure which was which, which was the original and which was the copy.

For a long time it was enough to be there as a spectator looking at the outside, walking around, seeing the planes, the contours, the shaped mass, but she knew that sooner or later she'd have to go inside. The barrier was permeable. She was too much of a coward not to do what she had come for. She took Bob Dexter's key from her pocket, went up to the Norman archway and tried the lock. She struggled with the door, couldn't tell if she was locking it or unlocking it, but something clicked and it swept open. The door felt light and lacking in substance, but that seemed appropriate, a sign that she was welcome here.

She entered the Cardboard House and found herself in the hall, taller and narrower than she'd have imagined, with rising, converging walls that met high above her to form a sloping, trapezoid skylight of gold and pewter-coloured glass. The ecclesiastical effect was not wasted on her, but underfoot she felt gravel and rubble and in a corner were a couple of crushed beer cans. Well, she could hardly be surprised, could hardly expect that in all these years somebody's curiosity hadn't brought them this way; tough young boys perhaps with their girlfriends, having their first alcohol, their first joints, their first sex. Her father would no doubt have approved, and she couldn't feel too bad about it either. What else were houses for?

She went into the living room. It was big and tranquil. One undulating glass wall opened on to the desert, and overhead a glass dome gazed up at the clear sky. It was a room she felt she could be content in. Some of the furniture was still in place, a sofa and chairs recognizable from the photographs in Dexter's portfolio. There were even books on the table and a pile of old newspapers. She found that a little creepy, as though something had been interrupted, as in an architectural Mary Celeste. She felt too a sense of the people who had previously lived here, Dexter and his family, and she was becoming aware of how much she wanted the place to be hers alone, to have always been hers, just waiting for her arrival.

Then, as she returned to the hall she saw through into a back room, one with an oval window and a sloping ceiling made out of galvanized iron, and her eyes picked out a bundle of rags in the corner, some dirty clothes, a thinly quilted sleeping bag. She went to the threshold of the room, peered in and saw a pair of old sneakers and a transistor radio and a plastic tumbler half full of dusty water. There was another pile of newspapers right there by the door and she picked up the top copy, looked at the headline and the date. Oh fuck. It was three days old. She was standing on the brink of someone's improvised bedroom. Someone was sleeping in her father's house. Who? She tried to imagine. Some old tramp or old hippie. A crazed junkie? A moody loner? Well, why not? This was America, after all. But why was she trying to work out his identity? What did it matter? The mere fact of invasion was enough to send her running out through the door.

Dexter was sitting on a rock halfway between the truck and the house. The speed of Kelly's exit told him something was wrong. He got to his feet and ran towards her, a sight she didn't find especially reassuring.

'What is it? What's up?' he shouted, a little over-dramatically it seemed to her, and she could hear the protectiveness, the fierce concern in his voice, his willingness to try to fix things, but she had no faith in that either.

'Someone's been living here,' she said. 'In fact, it looks like they still are.'

Dexter assimilated the information quickly and started checking the ground around the house as if looking for clues, and indeed there were footprints and what looked like bicycle tracks.

'OK, so we'll wait for him,' Dexter said. 'We'll have a little house-warming party.'

He had quickly become the aggressor rather than the protector. It was his territory that had been invaded, his pride that was affected. He went inside, in search of more clues, and after the briefest reconnoitre returned. He said nothing at all this time but went back to the rock he'd been sitting on, and Kelly saw no option but to join him. They waited

187

an hour or more in the hot, dry wind, doing and saying nothing, absorbing the silence.

They saw their man coming from a long way off, an angular, tattered desert rat on a mountain bike. His progress through the difficult terrain was slow but measured. He looked relentless. There was a bandanna round his forehead and a flag waving from the handlebars of the bike. And he was waving too, a bony arm reaching out in their direction. It was a gesture of ambiguous welcome. To be out here in this patch of desert ostensibly gave them a common purpose, but it also brought them into a dangerous proximity. He didn't want to appear threatening but neither did he want to be threatened.

He was not young. His skin was leathered and shrunk by the sun, pulled tight round the bones of his unshaven face, an old man's face, but his long hair was bleached by the sun and without grey, and when he got close and swung down from the saddle of his bike, his body and the way he carried himself were fit and loose.

'Please don't do anything crazy, will you?' Kelly whispered to Dexter.

'Like what? Beat the scumbag's brains out with a rock? No, I'll leave that to you.'

The man let his mountain bike fall over in the dirt and he walked up to them, in a display of exaggerated casualness.

'You here for the tour of the house?' he asked eagerly. 'I only charge a token fee. I normally ask five dollars, but if you're really hurtin' we can negotiate.'

Kelly thought at first this must be a wry, California desert joke, an oblique way of asking them what the hell they were doing on what he no doubt thought of as his domain, but he carried on talking and there was nothing wry about him.

'I don't get too many visitors out here,' he said, 'but the

188

ones who make the effort are always impressed. Some people look at this place and say it must have been built by aliens. I tell 'em they're wrong. I say it was built by a visionary.'

Neither Kelly nor Dexter wanted to argue about that. The stranger's good opinion of the house was disarming.

'Some folks say it's an eyesore. I say it's a fuckin' work of art. Some others say they like it but they wouldn't want to live in it. I say that's OK 'cos they're not gonna get the chance.'

He laughed too long and too shrilly at his own joke, trying to encourage Dexter and Kelly to join in. He looked bemused rather than disappointed when they didn't.

'What's your name?' Dexter asked.

'They call me Buster,' the man said and he found that funny too. 'So you want the tour or not?'

'Sure,' said Dexter. 'Why not?'

Kelly gave a low yelp of alarm. She'd been expecting something very different from Dexter though she didn't know what. It was surprising to find that at this moment, of all possible moments, he was prepared to hold back and see what developed, not to look for an instant solution. She watched him take a ten dollar bill from his pocket and hand it over. Their prospective tour guide received it and fastidiously folded it in half, then into quarters, into eighths and sixteenths, and then slipped it into the top of his sock.

'OK, let's go,' he said, and he moved towards the house with Dexter in his wake. Kelly was reluctant to go back, but staying outside while the two men went in would have been intolerable.

'Step right up,' said the man. 'You'll have to forgive me for the state of the place. The maid hasn't been here in days. They say a man needs a maid, but I figure all he needs is a strong right hand.'

Even then she knew it was going to end in trouble, though

she didn't know how far away that end might be. She suspected that humouring this man was not going to help much, and the longer Dexter remained passive the more fearful she became. But at least she got to see the rest of the house.

'You know, when I first moved in,' the man said, 'I figured I'd do something about them walls, you know, paint some murals, stick up some posters and brighten up the joint. But the longer I been here the less I felt inclined. Now I figure it's best leave well enough alone.'

'That's a great philosophy,' said Dexter.

'It's a pretty good house to live in,' Buster continued. 'It can get pretty hot and the air don't circulate too well, and if it ever rains which, let's face it, it don't do too often, the roof leaks like a sieve. But that's the price you pay for living in a national treasure.'

He took them from room to room: to the kitchen, from which all the appliances had been removed; to those bedrooms he wasn't using; to the sunken, purple-tiled bathroom; to a wedge-shaped study and out on to a shaded, jagged-edged balcony. Kelly observed it all intently, as though she might have to sketch it later, or give a description of the scene of the crime. This was not how she would have chosen to see the house, how she would ever have dreamed she'd be seeing it.

She found herself looking at details that were too small to have been included in the model: the light switches, the door handles, the taps. She tried hard to shut out the presence of their guide but she couldn't quite succeed. At times he prattled on about balance and proportion, the ingenious use of materials, about the way the sun moved through each room. Much of it sounded perfectly rational; but at times he became more disturbingly personal and anecdotal.

'It's a good house to get drunk in, a good house to get

stoned it. Yep, I admit it, I've imbibed and ingested and even inhaled in this house. It'd be a real good place to have parties in, 'cept I don't know nobody and nobody wants to know me. How about you folks? Want to party? Want to get high?'

'No,' said Dexter.

'Pity. And another thing, it's a great house for being naked in,' he said. 'You move around and the sun hits your body and it feels great. And it's a great house for jerking off in. You lie on your back and look up at all the weird angles and the way the light shines in, or you look out of a window at the sky and the clouds and you come like a train. Fact is, I must have jerked off about a hundred times in each and every room in this house. What do you think about that?'

Kelly felt he was trying to provoke her, trying to desecrate her father's house, and yet he couldn't know it was her father's house. The prospect of this unlovely man wandering naked from room to room and masturbating wasn't exactly appealing, but it was too pathetic and laughable to be genuinely offensive.

'I said what do you think of that?'

'I think that's not at all surprising,' Kelly replied.

'So how long have you been living here?' asked Dexter.

'As long as I can remember.'

'And how long's that?'

The man pretended to be racking his memory.

'You know, I forget,' and he laughed too hard again.

'Do you own this place?' Dexter persisted.

'I sure do. And the land all around it. Everything you can see from the house is mine.'

'Is that right?' said Dexter.

'I know I don't look much like a landowner, but that's because I'm a rich eccentric.'

191

'And tell me, who designed this house?'

'Designed?' the man said, not quite grasping the idea that a house might need to be designed.

'I mean, who was the architect?'

The man stuck his chin out and said heroically and proudly, 'Me, man. I did it all.'

Dexter grimaced, looked serious. Kelly feared the worst.

'OK, here's the deal,' Dexter said. 'I realize you've been out in the sun too long, and apart from a little trespassing I don't see that you've done anything too terrible here, but, the fact is, you know and I know this house isn't yours. You have no right to be here. You didn't build it. You don't own it. And I happen to know who *does* own it: my family – and that's really about all there is to it. So I'm going to give you about ten minutes to pick up your stuff and ride your bike out of here. OK? Do you have any problem with that?'

The man looked thoughtful and melancholy and his head swayed in a slack, floppy rhythm. 'Yeah, I guess I do have a problem with that,' he said, and somehow, from somewhere, he'd got a big black gun in his hand and he was pointing it at Dexter.

'Not again,' said Kelly.

But this time Dexter's reaction was very different. In fact he barely reacted at all. He backed away a little from the man but he appeared alarmingly at ease, unafraid, and quietly resigned, as though he'd lost some tiny, insignificant argument and was perfectly happy to accept the fact.

'It's OK,' Dexter said. 'I hear you. We're out of here.'

He turned as casually as could be, offering his back as a target and, without looking at Kelly he walked from the house. She felt stranded but Dexter was clearly her lifeline, and although she was unable to shrug off the stranger and

192

his gun in quite the way Dexter had appeared to, she followed his orderly withdrawal. The man stood in the doorway and watched them walk away. They had just about got to the truck when he fired his gun. He shot straight up in the air, and the desert space and silence absorbed the worst of its blast but it was enough to send Dexter and Kelly bolting, panicking, into the cab of the truck. The rush of adrenalin converted itself into engine noise and acceleration, and Dexter powered away from the house, everything loose and uncoordinated, the truck barely under control. Only then did he feel free to be angry. He was cursing to himself, partly taking his fury out on the desert road and the truck's suspension, and partly on Kelly.

'OK, so I didn't do anything crazy,' he shouted. 'That make you happy, did it?'

'Not especially,' said Kelly. 'But it wasn't a situation where I was likely to be very happy, was it?'

Dexter grunted and punched the boss of the steering wheel.

'But you could drive a little slower,' she said. 'That would make me happy.'

Dexter said, 'Fuck it,' and slammed on the brakes. The pick-up slewed across the road, almost went out of control, then righted itself.

Kelly felt sick, scared, excited. She was still strapped into the rollercoaster, the belt was stuck, she couldn't get out and was going round for the third, fourth, fifth time.

'I guess we can call the police and get rid of him,' Dexter said. 'Breaking and entering, criminal damage, trespass, threatening somebody with a gun. Even out here in the desert they take that stuff pretty seriously. This is still California, after all.'

'The Suffolk of America,' said Kelly.

193

After they'd driven a few miles in the direction of Frontier Town Dexter stopped the truck dead and sat still, taking deep lungfuls of the hot air, his hands hung over the top of the wheel. Kelly looked at him with some sympathy. She was impressed by his weakness, his uncertainty. She said, 'As a matter of fact, I don't think we should call the police.'

'Is that so?'

'It doesn't seem right somehow. I came here wanting something very personal, very private. I don't want it turning into cops and robbers. I don't want the police crawling all over my house.'

'*Whose* house? Whose fucking house?'

'Oh shit. Did I really say that? My *father's* house. *Your* father's house. *Your* house, I suppose. Oh shit.'

Dexter laughed. He enjoyed her confusion, and that changed his mood, burnt off some of the fog of anger.

'So, do you have any bright ideas?' he asked.

'Maybe we could go back later and talk to him again.'

'Yeah. Right. Nothing he'd like better than a fireside chat.'

'Or,' said Kelly, 'we could go get a beer. Or three.'

'Kelly, am I bringing you down to my level?'

'I was already down at your level, I'm afraid.'

The Rocket Saloon had filled up. There was a group of young guys with long hair and khaki shorts and one of them was absent-mindedly playing a guitar. There were a few middle-aged men who might once have been Hell's Angels. They'd kept their Harleys and their beards but had lost their power to disturb and now looked like freakish but avuncular old cowboys. There was a trio of airmen with razored haircuts and shades, and there were other, less identifiable, stragglers whose presence seemed as inexplicable as Kelly's and Dexter's; maybe tourists, maybe people who liked to make a visit to this bar an excuse for driving through the desert. Kelly didn't feel at home exactly but she didn't feel conspicuously out of place either. People regarded her with the same degree of interest that she regarded them; local colour, if not necessarily from this locale.

'Welcome to America,' said Dexter. 'Beer, motels, guns.'

'Something tells me this isn't quite your America, Dexter.'

'It's as much mine as it is anybody else's.'

Kelly pressed her beer bottle to her forehead and let her skin leave its imprint on the condensation of the wet glass.

'What are we going to do, Dexter? What are we going to do?'

'I have a great idea,' said Dexter. 'Let's finish our drinks, go to our respective motel rooms, get a good night's sleep, then in the morning drive back to LA.'

'And then?'

'Then nothing. That's it. We leave things exactly as they are. You wanted to see the house and you've seen it. OK, so there's some old weirdo living in it, but so what? He's not hurting it. In lots of ways it's probably better with him in it. It's not like you were planning to live there, were you?'

Of course not. Of course she wasn't. Or was she? Maybe in some idiotic way that was what had been in her mind all along. Perhaps a part of her wanted to move in and be the curator of the Cardboard House, having renamed it the Christopher Howell Foundation or something like that; a sophisticated roadside attraction, a sort of museum, where she could show visitors her father's glorious achievement, much like 'Buster' had done, without the masturbatory references but with the bonus of her family connection.

No, she didn't really want that, not in the real world. In the real world she wanted a life of her own, not a life that was a footnote to her father's. But she would have liked to have it as an option, to be in the house; not living in it, not staying in it, not necessarily making it hers, but just being able to be there. She knew she had no rights, moral or otherwise, and she didn't much want Buster arrested or punished, but she wished he wasn't there, had never been there.

'It's a reasonable idea,' she said, 'but I think I have a better one.'

'Oh really?'

'Yes. How about we get gradually and thoroughly ratted and then go back to one or other of our motel rooms and drunkenly shag our brains out. For old times' sake, or something.'

Dexter swigged his beer.

'OK,' he said. 'Not the final solution but OK.'

It didn't take too long. A few more beers and a few whisky chasers later, having bought a handful of bottles to take back with them, they were in Kelly's room and she was staring up at the crevices of the motel ceiling while Dexter toiled on top of her. Drunken sex, any sex, with Dexter had seemed inconceivable when she first decided to come with him to America, but plans were made to be changed, and now it seemed as though it had always been inevitable; not meaningful, perhaps, not exactly enjoyable, but somehow unavoidable. At that moment she needed to be in touch with someone so as not to feel utterly alone and defeated; and if Dexter was not the one she'd have chosen given an entire world of possibilities, then what were the alternatives – picking up someone in the bar? That would have been no good, and it would certainly have pissed off Dexter, and even though there had been times when pissing off Dexter had seemed a worthwhile pursuit, right now she wanted him on her side.

The bed was wide and ridged. Under the bottom sheet there was a layer of thick transparent plastic, protecting the mattress against spillages. It creaked thickly beneath her.

She thought of all the people who had slept in this bed, all the people who'd fucked on it, come on it, drunk beer in it. She wondered if her father had even stayed in this very room – the odds weren't bad given the size of the motel – and had he really behaved badly like he said in the article, or was that just creative licence? And how precisely did she feel about that? She knew that fathers were allowed to be imperfect and, in any case, what exactly was supposed to constitute fatherly perfection? Chastity? Incorruptibility? Infallibility? The old, impossible values? But she wished he'd been a little less conspicuous in his imperfections.

Dexter was fucking her harder and faster now, sweating, getting ready to lose control. She put her hands round his neck and shoulders, holding on until this latest fairground ride was over. She knew she wouldn't be sharing his abandon; too much beer, too much on her mind, but she enjoyed his enthusiasm and passion, and was glad that he seemed so eager for her. The bed twanged and Dexter came and then he slipped away and was quiet and heavy beside her and he immediately drifted off into sleep. She knew she was supposed to hate that sort of thing, but she really didn't. She reached for the remote control, bracketed to the bedside table, and turned on the television.

She got herself another beer and shuffled through the channels, through the wash of food and car commercials, old sitcoms, a shopping channel, country and western videos. She was amused and appalled, simultaneously bored and overstimulated, wanting to be engrossed in something but wanting to search further through the mash of faces and voices and images. It seemed to be meaningless. She *wanted* it to be meaningless, and then suddenly there was some ridiculous commercial, she wasn't even sure what it was for, life insurance or low-fat spread or a mail-order catalogue, something bland and inoffensive, but it showed a father and a young daughter in a rose garden and they were holding hands, and the father leaned over and kissed the little girl's head, and suddenly Kelly began to lose it.

She propped herself up on the bed, crying quietly at first, but before long the crying got louder and louder, and her body began to quiver. She knew she was getting out of hand, sobbing, making a noise and a vibration that could shake walls.

Dexter woke up, and in a blurred, inept voice asked if she was all right. 'No, I'm fucking not,' she said, and even though Dexter must surely have been aware that nothing he could do or say was likely to make the slightest difference, he still tried. A hand, an arm, a shoulder, were all offered and rejected, and Kelly rolled away from him, over to the far edge of the bed. Dexter sat up, exasperated.

'You're going to tell me this is another one of those things I can't fix, right?'

'You're so fucking perceptive, Dexter.'

He got up wearily, sadly, from the bed, and put on enough clothes so that he could leave her and go back to his own room. He closed the door behind him, almost a slam, though not quite, just enough to signal that he wanted her to feel bad for having rejected him, for having spurned his offer of comfort, but she couldn't be bothered with all that stuff, not now. Once he'd gone something changed and lightened. She was alone, and empty, not quite whole but not quite ruined, damaged but not destroyed. In the circumstances she'd settle for that.

12

She woke next morning with the blurred pulse of a hangover running through her head, and she lay still for a long time, clutching the sheet to her. Her joints were stiff and her body felt beaten up. The smell of Dexter was on her. She was experiencing no remorse but she felt horribly scuffed and shop-worn. The day lay ahead of her, a parade of unknown terrors, random episodes that might involve another visit to the Cardboard House, negotiation with the crazed house-sitter, trying to get the police interested, terrible hassles, confrontations, guns, a shame-faced return to LA, another drunken night in the Rocket Saloon, or any combination of these things, or none of them.

There was a tentative knock on the motel door, and she knew it had to be Dexter. She felt no animosity towards him this morning. She kept the sheet around herself and let him in. He was carrying two small polystyrene cups of coffee. Kelly took one and grunted her thanks. She hoped he wouldn't try to touch her or kiss her, but she had made her point. He kept his distance, sat quietly on the edge of the bed, demanding nothing. He seemed calmer than she'd ever seen him.

'If I have anything to be sorry for, then I'm sorry,' he said.

'You don't need to be sorry.'

'Good, because that's the way I see it too.'

'Been up long?' Kelly asked.

'Hours.'

'Got a hangover?'

'No. Have you?'

She nodded.

'They're serving breakfast in the saloon. It's as good a hangover cure as any.'

She wasn't sure it was exactly what she wanted, but she put on clothes and went along with it. There was nobody eating in the saloon when they arrived, but the tough cookie who'd been working behind the bar the previous night was there wiping down a table and laying out knives and forks. She motioned for them to sit down and handed over menus. She didn't smile or say anything, but she didn't seem particularly hostile. She was inert and self-contained and that suited Kelly. She and Dexter had nothing to say to each other either, and they sat in the morning gloom basking in the dim silence.

She was glad of Dexter's silence, glad to be free of plans and discussions. If anything needed to be said it didn't need to be said at this precise moment. Later would be fine. The day would unfold in its own time, with its own logic.

They had nearly finished breakfast before the spell was broken. A police car pulled up outside and two solid, khaki-uniformed officers walked into the saloon. Kelly looked at their guns and their sunglasses; the stuff of legend and television. They looked serious and threatening and larger than life but they joked with the waitress who almost gave them a smile, and they deposited themselves at a table across the other side of the room from Dexter and Kelly and ordered breakfast. The silence and equilibrium had been kicked out of the room.

'It's a real mess out there,' one of the police said.

'I figured,' said the waitress indifferently. 'Know how it happened?'

'I can guess. He was out of his head on something, booze or dope or both, and he passed out or fell over, dropped his cigarette or knocked over a candle or a kerosene lamp. Nothing we or anybody could do.'

'Get the body out yet?'

'What's left of it. Looked like something your cook had finished with.'

Kelly watched Dexter as he determinedly refused to react to what he was hearing. He finished his last piece of toast, sipped his coffee.

'Who owned that old hippie weirdo house anyway?'

'Some big shot in LA. Hasn't been there in years. He won't be vacationing there now, that's for sure.'

Dexter's eyes stayed securely on his plate. He didn't look up, didn't glance at Kelly or the police. He continued to act as if he had heard nothing, as if the police had been discussing something as trivial as a parking ticket. Kelly couldn't eat or drink, could barely swallow, certainly couldn't talk, but when Dexter had at last finished and when he silently pushed back his chair and got up from the table, she followed him out, knowing that he would get in the truck and drive out to the Cardboard House, or whatever was left of it.

They didn't speak on the way there. Dexter drove slowly, calmly. Certainly Kelly could see there was no rush, nothing that would change before they got there, but she still didn't understand his icy self-possession, his lack of urgency.

They could see the smoke rising long before they arrived. It was still wafting up from the wreckage in thin, dirty streaks.

201

There was one police car and a couple of unmarked vans parked beside the blackened, crumpled framework of the building. It looked crushed, stamped on. The Cardboard House had fallen in on itself, had been reduced to a mesh of loose, interlocking components. Kelly could still recognize sections of wall, roof, door and window, but they no longer made sense. The integrity of the building had gone. It had always been a house of fragments and discontinuity, now the fragments were united by a thick black tar that coated and held them.

Dexter parked beside the squad car but he and Kelly had barely stepped out of the truck before they were confronted by a policewoman, as big and formidable as either of the guys they'd seen having breakfast.

'Do you have any business here, sir?' she asked.

Dexter hesitated, and Kelly saw that if he was ever going to lay claim to the house, to his part in the action, this would have to be the moment. But he hesitated a little too long and the policewoman took that as a 'no', as an indication that they were only there to gawp, and she said, 'Then you should get back in your vehicle and drive on, sir. This ain't a tourist attraction.'

For a moment Kelly wanted to stay, to argue, to insist that she did have business there, that she belonged, but almost immediately she saw this was no longer true. What business could she have with a burnt-out building? How could she possibly belong? And how could she possibly explain anything at all to a female Californian cop in a khaki uniform with sunglasses and a gun?

Kelly and Dexter got into the truck, back on to the road that led through Frontier Town, that would eventually take them back to the freeway, back to Los Angeles. Kelly looked over her shoulder, through the dusty rear window of the

202

truck, watching the smouldering wreckage recede, become part of the desert landscape. Only after they'd been driving for an hour or so did they speak.

Dexter said, 'You see, sometimes things have a way of fixing themselves.'

Kelly said, 'I don't know if I believe that.'

13

Kelly told Dexter to drop her off at an airport hotel. She could have demanded that he simply put her on the next plane home, but she didn't, and it occurred to her that maybe she scared him by doing that. Perhaps he realized just how much trouble she could get him into if she told her story a certain way. He didn't try to dissuade or persuade her, but took her straight to a big, shining, personality-free hotel in sight of LAX and some long-term parking lots. He booked the room for her, let the desk clerk take his credit card and run it through the machine. He wanted to pay for everything, and Kelly couldn't see any reason to pay her own way, not now. He owed her a great deal. She saw relief in his face as she took the electronic key. Something was over and now she was obligated, now she was his. It was a significant parting. He said he'd be in touch, but Kelly wasn't interested. Once you'd stopped believing in a person the way Kelly had stopped believing in Dexter none of it mattered much. It seemed perfectly possible that she'd never hear from him or see him again.

The hotel was a place of spongy carpet, rattan chairs, elevator music that was not only in the elevator, a hotel bar with its Japanese crackers in minuscule bowls, men in lightweight suits who greeted each other too loudly, called each other 'buddy' and talked rapidly about deals in Baltimore and Phoenix and Portland.

Her hotel room was anonymously comforting. Its neutrality reassured her; the red laquered headboard and bedside cabinets, a big television on a multi-drawered sideboard. There was a mini-bar and room service, and she did her best to abuse both. She ate and drank in her room. She watched a movie channel. She bought a lot of magazines at the hotel shop. She showered frequently. She was alone in Los Angeles, so what should she do? Take the bus tour, visit Disneyland and Universal Studios? Should she try renting a car and drive around in a panic, feeling lost and threatened with nowhere to go? Should she hire a cab and ask the driver to show her the sights?

On the second day the phone rang. She ignored it. It wouldn't have mattered who was on the other end since she wasn't intending to speak to anybody at all. But she knew it had to be Dexter. He alone knew where she was, and he was still the last person she wanted to speak to. There was only one thing to say, only one question worth asking, one answer worth knowing: did he burn down the Cardboard House, and was it by accident or design, out of madness or anger or as another exercise in fixing? But there was no answer she would accept. She could never quite believe him if he said no, and if he said yes then the consequences were too terrible.

He left a message with the switchboard, asking her to call him, if and when she wanted to, in her own time, no hassle, no pressure. Easy to ignore. And then later the same day there was a message from Dexter's father, of a similarly low intensity, though she thought with a different meaning.

If nothing else the message must mean that somewhere

in all this Dexter had explained at least part of the story to his father. Would the account Dexter gave him be any more reliable than the one he'd have given her? Probably not, but as the owner of the house, Bob Dexter must surely have taken some action. Were the police on the case? Insurance investigators? Would they want to talk to her? Might Bob Dexter even make a profit out of the fire? Would he want to drive out and see the wreck for himself?

And what else would Dexter be doing? Hiding? Drinking? Writing his famous article about her, about Christopher Howell's failure of a daughter? Jesus, he'd certainly have enough material now; but would it be a scholarly footnote or a chunk of lurid gossip, a pathetic true confession? Something told her she would not get to read it. And yet that scenario of Dexter the architectural scholar or journalist didn't quite convince her. She found it easier to imagine him picking up the pieces of his old life, calling his ex-wife, being persuasive, saying everything would be different, that he was ready to make adjustments, to try again, try harder this time, that he wanted to go back into the family business, to do the right thing, to get serious. The wife would be reluctant at first, but then slowly she'd come round. She'd be so happy, so optimistic. So blonde.

Kelly thought of calling her mother. She too wanted a connection with her old life, her only life, a confirmation that not everything had been burnt to the ground. But naturally she didn't make the call. It would have been too hard, and she'd have been giving too much away. Her mother would have known something was wrong, and there was no way Kelly could spell out the details of that wrong. Sooner or preferably much later she would have to tell all; it was too big a secret to keep all to herself. But she couldn't do it now: not from here; not like this.

A silly regret went through her. She should have taken some photographs of the Cardboard House. Would that have preserved anything? Or should she have grabbed something more solid: a door handle, a lump of plaster? Would that have made her feel any better? Was there perhaps still time to get back to the desert, to the charred ruin and grab a piece of blackened window frame, a splinter of smoke-stained glass? Was that what she needed? Or did she just need a drink? Many drinks?

She got sick of her hotel room and her clean body, and she went down to the bar. She sat on a stool, a copy of *Vogue* set squarely in front of her, trying hard not to notice her surroundings. She had succeeded in not noticing the man sitting beside her, but he heard her accent as she ordered a vodka and tonic and he said, 'You're English.' Then she noticed him: a big man, soft with a fleshy face, big smooth expanses of thick, newly shaved jowls; an ugly man, a dull man, not at all dangerous, not at all attractive.

'Can I buy you a drink?' he asked.

'You can buy me a drink,' Kelly replied. 'But you can't fuck me.'

He considered the trade-off.

'That's what I like about the English, polite, reserved . . .'

But he bought her a drink, and after he'd given her some flannel about big deals involving designer jeans and Japan and some Industry people down in Culver City, he said, 'So if you're not planning to fuck anybody, why exactly are you sitting alone at the bar getting drunk?'

For one insane moment she thought of explaining everything, of letting this dull, inconsequential stranger be her confessor. It had a certain melodramatic appeal but she knew she couldn't do it, and she knew she couldn't give him a convincing answer. She got up from her stool and left the bar, took the lift back to her room. When she got there she found a slim, important-looking envelope leaning against the door. Cautiously, dubiously, she took the envelope, held it to her and made sure she was safely inside before opening the seal.

Inside the envelope was a sheet of headed notepaper, Bob Dexter Associates, with a couple of lines of big scrawled handwriting: 'Kelly, you should probably read this. Call me if you need to talk. Or just call me. Bob.' The 'this' in question was a bound folder of fifteen or so typed pages, an original manuscript, a little creased, a little tinged with age. The document was a letter to Bob Dexter written a long time ago, a letter from an architect to his client. She turned to the first page with more trepidation than hope.

London,
12 November 1969

Dear Bob,

I am back in England, back from the mania and mad aspiration of America, and I think have some apologies to make. I have built you a building and I know it's a failure. You, unfortunately, know it too. If one or other of us could deceive ourselves, either as blissfully happy, deluded client or as wounded, misunderstood, visionary, deluded architect there might be something to salvage from it all, but I suspect there isn't.

I know that politicians are told never to apologize and never explain, but as an architect, or at least a would-be architect, and now as a failed architect, I feel a pressing need to do both. Apologizing doesn't take long. I'm sorry. I'm sorry I wasted your time, money and materials. I'm sorry that I'm not a better architect, the one that both of us thought and hoped I was. I bit off more than I could chew. My design wasn't good enough. My handling of men and materials was incompetent. I'm sorry. Yes, apologizing is the easy part. Explaining is something different. What follows may seem like a crazed ramble, but at least I don't think you'll be able to dismiss it as self-justification.

You know, there's an argument that says all human activity is a brave slap in the face of chaos and oblivion. Simply to get out of bed in the morning and not abandon yourself to the forces of dissipation is a kind of triumph. All works of art, I think, are a kind of bridgehead against impending destruction but architecture seems to be a special case.

Most art forms can be abstract or hypothetical, yet a hypothetical building would seem to be an absurdity if not a contradiction in terms. A building that only exists as an abstraction in the architect's mind is no building at all, whereas a play, a novel, a piece of music can have an existence and a kind of integrity even if it's never performed, read or heard. There's always some possibility that poets who never publish or painters who never exhibit will be discovered after their deaths, since even if unacknowledged and unknown their works do actually exist. But an architect who does not build is no architect at all. The plan of a building is not the equivalent of a musical score or a set of stage directions. Architecture is the art of the real and the concrete, in several senses, only some of them ironic.

I've heard it said that the first thing the aspiring architect needs to have is rich and indulgent parents. Since I don't have those, you took on the role instead.

Thank you for being indulgent, at least for a while. Sorry if I have made you less rich.

There are not many boy geniuses in the world of architecture, there is no Mozart, and yet Bruce Goff came close. He was born in 1904. By 1916 he was working in an architect's office. By 1918 he'd had a design published, and by 1919 one of his designs was being built. By the age of twenty-one he'd designed twenty-five buildings, and twelve of these were eventually constructed. You have to be impressed. My favourite Bruce Goff design however is the unbuilt Cowboy Hall of Fame, for Oklahoma City. It consists of six more or less discrete buildings each of them in the shape of a horseshoe. It's clever, funny, silly and (I suppose you would have to say) kitsch.

Goff, incidentally or not, was a homosexual and was arrested and charged with 'encouraging a fourteen-year-old boy to become delinquent by . . . looking upon, touching, mauling and feeling his body'. Goff pleaded guilty. Today there are those who celebrate him as a creator of 'queer space'.

Frank Lloyd Wright, as a matter of fact, briefly faced charges of white slavery for transporting his Montenegrin mistress across the Wisconsin/Minnesota state line, but the case never came to anything. The mistress's husband decided Wright wasn't such a villain after all.

I sometimes like to think that the language of architectural description has a lot in common with the language of sex. There are moments when this seems very significant and moments when it does not. It's almost invariably a compliment to describe a building as 'sensuous'. One has often heard 'virile' as a term of architectural approbation, 'effete' as a term of abuse. 'Camp' is even worse.

There are some words that appear, more or less accidentally to be *double entendres*; words like trusses, buttresses, groins, but perhaps this is only to say that the body and buildings can be described in the same vocabulary.

We all know the expression, almost impossible to use seriously any more, 'my body is a temple' and we all know what it means. I've never heard anyone say their body was an Anderson shelter or a multi-storey car park or a burger bar, although these are all structures with certain virtues that a body might happily share. On the other hand people are always referring to their bodies as wrecks and ruins.

When we look at the face or body of an ageing but once beautiful woman, what exactly are we seeing? Is it just wrinkles and old skin? Are we simply seeing the effects of time and decay on the fabric of the body? Or are we seeing our own memories of what that face and body once looked like? We look at the fifty-year-old Bette Davis or Tallulah Bankhead and we are reminded of the twenty-year-old version. We view the ruin and we mentally reconstruct the unruined version. And is this perhaps what we do when we view the Colosseum or the Acropolis? We see through the ruin. The ruin helps us to know the early version, the earlier perfection.

I suppose the process is somewhat different for men. True, we may feel a certain nostalgia for the ruined good looks of, say, Orson Welles, but when we look at the older Robert Mitchum or John Wayne we seldom feel much nostalgia for the younger, less craggy versions.

Their patina suits them. They seem to have become more themselves, a sort of Mount Rushmore in the flesh. A female equivalent is inconceivable.

Ultimately, however, Mount Rushmore is subject to the same erosive forces as any other man-made thing. I happen to love ruins, but I know that for a ruin to have meaning it must once have been something we would prefer not to see ruined. The piles of stone that once were Nineveh or Babylon are poignant because the places they remind us of were once infinitely so much more than just a pile of stones. A pile of stones that once was Milton Keynes would have far less melancholy splendour.

On the outskirts of Paris there's an estate known as the Desert de Retz. Built on it is what looks like a broken, fluted column of massive dimensions, sixty-five feet in diameter and perhaps ninety feet high. From its proportions we can see that if the column were complete it would be hundreds of feet tall. The building of which it was a part, a temple, no doubt, would be inhumanly vast, a place where gargantuans worshipped.

But, of course, this column is all too human, and it was never a part of any whole building, and, strangely enough for a column, it has windows. In fact what we're dealing with here is a folly built in the late eighteenth century by Chevalier François Racine de Monville. It was a six-storey dwelling with its rooms laid out in layers round a central spiral staircase.

It's been used intermittently over the centuries by its various owners, and in an attempt to make it look less like a ruined column and more like a tower, one of them decided to straighten off the roof line so that it lost its jagged, broken appearance. That seems to me to have been an act of moronic incomprehension, trying to unruin a ruin. But time has won a small victory here. Cracks have appeared, chunks of masonry have fallen away from the building, ivy has crawled up and around its walls. It is now uninhabited, possibly uninhabitable. What began as a fake ruin has now become a genuine ruin.

On 27 March 1963, Richard Neutra's Silverlake Studio, known as the Van der Leeuw Research House, was virtually destroyed by an electrical fire. Photographs show little remaining except a blackened shell. The house had contained almost all of Neutra's archive: correspondence, plans and drawings, slides and negatives, scrapbooks, his architectural prizes and awards, personal memorabilia; and it all went up in flames. Neutra and his wife Dione were in the mid-West at the time of the fire and they flew back to look at the wreckage. 'Everything is gone,' his wife wrote a little later. 'The past is finished.' But Neutra looked at the burnt-out shell for all of five seconds, then began discussing ways of rebuilding and improving the house. I guess that's what a real architect would do. I have to say that over the last few months I've wished that the Cardboard House would burn down and release us all.

I'm no Richard Neutra, I'm afraid, but I suspect we already knew that. At this moment I really don't know who I am at all, who I was trying to be, who my heroes or influences are. I always find it ridiculous when architects say how much they've been influenced by Michelangelo and Lutyens and Sir John Soane and Sir John Vanbrugh and Michele Sanmicheli and Donato

214

Bramante and Luis Barragan and Le Corbusier and
Alberti and Borromini and Alvar Aalto and Palladio.
What could it possibly mean to be 'influenced' by those
people? Any self-respecting architect who had a sense of
that crowd looking over his shoulder while he was
trying to create a building shouldn't be 'influenced', he
should be absolutely paralysed.

I think of Lloyd Wright, the son of Frank Lloyd
Wright. He's a rather good architect. He's no Frank
Lloyd Wright, but then who is? Fortunately most
architects don't have to live up to quite that sort of
direct comparison, but poor Lloyd, being the son, does.
Perhaps, however, his greatest achievement, and the
thing for which he'll be best remembered, is inventing
the Lincoln Logs toy construction set. I can't decide if
this is a tragedy or not.

I find myself thinking of Jesse Winchester, begetter of
the Winchester House in San Jose. She was the
daughter-in-law of the inventor of the Winchester rifle,
and after her father-in-law and her husband had died,
and after having enjoyed the spoils of the Winchester
fortune for a great many years, she consulted a psychic
in the belief that she needed protecting from the ghosts
of those killed by Winchester rifles.

Perhaps she simply had a building mania, was a sort
of Californian Bess of Hardwick, and needed a
justification, but whatever the reason, the psychic
helped her to believe that she would be safe from the
dead while ever the house she was building remained
'unfinished'. And so Jesse began an open-ended building
programme that had incompletion as its chief objective.

There are a hundred and sixty rooms in the
Winchester House, thirteen bathrooms, forty staircases –

most of them with thirteen steps – though not all of them actually leading anywhere; sometimes they simply ascend to a blank wall. There are Tiffany stained-glass windows in places where the sun never shines. The official guided tour, rather less fun than expected when I went on it, involves a one-mile trail through some but by no means all the house's rooms.

Ultimately, I don't know whether Jesse Winchester was a dupe or a paranoiac or just an eccentric, but I know enough about houses and their construction to realize it's quite easy not to finish them. The world is full of home builders who never quite get round to making those few final, all-important finishing touches. If Jesse Winchester had simply wanted to leave her house 'unfinished' surely she need only have left a corner of the bathroom untiled or one ceiling unpainted.

Certainly there were those who might have wished that the Taj Mahal had never been finished. Personally, I've always found the Taj Mahal a fairly objectionable building, not least because it's so self-regardingly pretty, so full of itself. But there are other objections. Shah Jahan built it for his favourite wife, but only as a tomb after she'd died. Wouldn't it have been more touching if he'd built it for her while she was alive? More objectionable still, once the building was complete Jahan had all the craftsmen who'd worked on it killed because he wanted to make sure they didn't go off and build something better elsewhere.

The desire to kill builders and workmen, and indeed architects, is an entirely natural one, one that we both understand after our experiences on the Cardboard House, but it still seems a little unnecessary. And it reminds me of the old joke about the English bricklayer who visits the Egyptian Pyramids, and the tour guide tells him they were built by the Pharaohs, and the bricklayer says, 'I'll bet the bloody Pharaoh never so much as lifted a brick.' I mean, if Shah Jahan had really wanted to make sure nothing better was ever built he should have killed himself, because he was the true begetter of the Taj Mahal. Without him there'd have been no building at all.

You know, sometimes I think the whole point of architecture is to create something cold, pure and chaste. But then I think that humanity isn't cold, pure and chaste, so why on earth should humanity's buildings be that way?

Humanity is often crass, flawed, damaged, and no doubt we get the buildings we deserve, and although I suspect no architect can deliberately set out to make a crass, flawed, damaged building; undoubtedly many of them can do it by instinct. And when I think of cold, pure, chaste buildings, what I actually find myself thinking of is an igloo, a serviceable structure but not the greatest architectural achievement imaginable. But igloos do have at least one advantage over most buildings, certainly over the crass, flawed and damaged variety; when they've served their purpose they melt harmlessly away. Today I certainly wish the Cardboard House would do the same.

Trying to make buildings is a hard, hard job; too hard for me, obviously. I think I'd rather be a William Dowsing, an iconoclast. I'd rather like to go through the world destroying the things I don't like: the unnecessary decoration, the graven images, the icons, the trademarks. You could turn it into an ideology if you wanted, into a system, but basically I'd do it because it felt good, because it suited my personality. It would be a worthwhile job, a clean job, and I know exactly where I'd start.

I can understand why some people are unhappy at living too closely with the prospect of oblivion, but others seem to find it curiously undisturbing. People build their houses at the base of volcanoes, on flood plains, on fault lines, next to nuclear power stations. It may be a lack of imagination or a silly belief that it can't happen to them, but I prefer to think they do it because they enjoy thumbing their noses at the inevitability of extinction.

As I said at the beginning, I have made some mistakes, and I'm genuinely sorry. But don't worry, Bob. It'll never happen again. I'll make sure of that.

Sincerely,
Christopher Howell.

She had barely finished reading the letter when the phone rang. This time she answered it, and Bob Dexter was on the other end, his voice sounding close and deep and, yes, fatherly.

'So now you know,' he said.

'What do I know?'

'If I have to tell you then I guess maybe you *don't* know.'

'Why didn't you give me the letter when I saw you?'

'You didn't need a letter then. You had the house itself.'

'And now that it's gone a letter's supposed to be a substitute?'

'It's not supposed to be anything.'

It could have sounded antagonistic coming from someone else, but Bob Dexter was calm, serene, unthreatening. She wanted to cause a ripple in the smooth finish of him, but she doubted she could.

'How's Dexter?' she asked.

'He's pretty upset. He feels responsible. He feels guilty.'

'Yes?'

'Sure. He thinks he should have done something. If he'd kicked the guy out of the house that afternoon, then the guy wouldn't have been able to get drunk and set fire to the place.'

So that was the story. How reassuring.

'And what do *you* think?'

'I think guilt's a very wasteful emotion.'

'Have you talked to the police?'

'Well, they've talked to me. They found I was the owner of the house. They told me it had burnt down. Pretty decent of them.'

'Do they want to talk to me?'

He waited just a beat too long before saying, 'As far as the police are concerned you were never there. You and Dexter were never there.'

'Very convenient.'

'Why would you want it to be inconvenient?'

She let it go. What was the point? Who did she need to convince?

'You all right, Kelly? You need anything? Money? Anything?'

'No. I'm flying back to England tomorrow. I've decided.'

'That's good. But you don't need to. You could stick around if you wanted, do some sightseeing. Go bowling or whatever. If you need a guide then I'd be more than happy.'

'I won't be needing a guide.'

'That's fine. But if you need me you know where I am.'

'Why would I need you?'

She needed a drink, another in a long series. Maybe she needed other things too: some good dope, a good man, a good mother, a good father substitute, but they weren't on offer in the hotel or anywhere else as far as she could tell. Above all she needed not to be alone.

She looked at herself in the mirror, put on a little too much make-up and left her room. She was alone in the lift and its descent seemed endless. So now she knew. Her father had been a failure, a failed architect, and he hadn't liked that, so he'd wiped the failure from the record and become something else. That didn't seem so reprehensible. It was all right to fail – perhaps it was inevitable – and after you'd failed you picked yourself up and moved on to the next thing. You told a few lies, blurred a few realities. But what if that failed too? What if you kept free-falling, waiting to hit a bottom that never came?

The lift doors opened and she walked through the lobby into the bar. There were a couple of single men there, but the man with the soft face – her potential confessor – had gone. She ordered a drink and threw back a handful of Japanese crackers. The alcohol would soon be doing its work in her system. She'd be feeling better, more blurred. She'd be feeling less. Then she'd be falling into conversation with some man, hearing him talk about his job, his car, his home town, very pointedly not talking about his wife or children. Yes, he'd be getting lucky tonight. He'd be feeling good about himself. He never realized he had so much charm. And sooner or later they'd be in bed, Kelly staring up at another ceiling, feeling blank and fucked and obliterated, just what she wanted, and then tomorrow she'd fly back to England. She'd become a taxi driver again. She'd still be

220

herself and she'd still have a life. Things would be different but they wouldn't be over.

And she tried to tell herself that the destruction of the Cardboard House didn't really matter all that much. A house wasn't a castle. It wasn't fortified or impregnable. It was only a place to live, something inanimate. You projected your feelings on to it, but that was all it was; projection, pretence. A house was just inert building materials arranged with greater or lesser degrees of skill, with only the meanings and desires you brought to it.

She knocked back her drink and ordered another. She didn't feel so bad. She made eye contact with a man on the other side of the bar. For the first time in a long time she felt completely in control. She didn't feel remotely ruined.